First Fam'lies

OF THE

SIERRAS.

By JOAQUIN MILLER,

Author of "Songs of the Sierras," "Songs of the Sun-Lands," "The Ship in the Desert," Etc.

CHICAGO:
JANSEN, McCLURG & CO.
1876.

LAKESIDE
PUBLISHING & PRINTING CO.
CHICAGO.

TO

MY OLD

COMPANION IN ARMS,

PRINCE JAMIE TOMAS,

OF

LEON, NICARAGUA.

CONTENTS.

PAGE.

In the Forks, - - - - - - 5

Little Billie Piper, - - - - 15

The First Woman in the Forks, - 21

Sunday in the Sierras, - - - - - 31

Washee-Washee, - - - - - 40

Some Unwritten History, - - - 62

That Boy, - - - - - - 69

Sandy's Courtship, - - - - - 74

"That Boy" is Ill, - - - - 78

A Scene in the Sierras, - - - 84

The Parson's Pursuit of Love, - - 90

Grit, - - - - - - - - - 100

An Announcement, - - - - - 110

A Wedding in the Sierras, - - - 118

What's the Matter Now? - - - 124

Was the Woman Insane? - - - 136

Captain Tommy, - - - - - - 149

"Blood!" - - - - - - - 157

PAGE.
How did it Happen? - - - - - 164
A Flag of Truce, - - - - - - 174
The Question None Could Answer, - 183
Debatable Ground, - - - - - - 194
Another Wedding at the Forks, - 200
The Judge is Lonesome, - - - - 211
After the Deluge — What then? - 215
The Widow in Disgrace, - - - 219
Billie Piper and Deboon, - - - 224
The Gopher, - - - - - - - 229
A Natural Death, - - - - - 234
A Funeral, - - - - - - - 239
The Caravan of Death, - - - 251
The End, - - - - - - - 255

FIRST FAM'LIES OF THE SIERRAS.

CHAPTER I.

IN THE FORKS.

NOW there was young Deboon from Boston, who was a very learned man. He was in fact one of those fearfully learned men. He was a man who could talk in all tongues—and think in none.

Perhaps he had sometime been a waiter.

I am bound to say that the most dreadfully learned young men I have ever met are the waiters in the Continental hotels.

Besides that he was very handsome. He was, indeed, almost as handsome as a French barber, or a first-class steward.

Another thing that helped to defeat him in this hurried election was his love of animals and his dislike of hard work. The handsome fellow stood for election this day with a bushy-tailed squirrel frisking on his shoulder, and a pair of pink-eyed white mice peeping out like a handkerchief from the pocket of his red shirt.

Then there was Chipper Charley — smart enough, and a man, too, who had read at least a dozen books; but the Forks did n't want him for an Alcalde any more than it did Deboon.

Then there was Limber Tim, and Limber certainly could write his name, for he was always leaning up against trees and houses and fences, when he could find them, and writing the day and date, and making grotesque pictures with a great carpenter's pencil, which he carried in the capacious depths of his duck breeches' pocket. But when Sandy proposed Limber Tim, the Camp silently but firmly shook its head, and said, "Not for Joseph."

At last the new camp pitched upon a man who, it seemed, had been called The Judge from the first. Perhaps he had been born with that name. It would indeed have been hard to think of him under any other appellation whatever. It had been easier to imagine that when he had first arrived on earth his parents met him at the door, took his carpet-bag, called him Judge, and invited him in.

As is usually the case in the far, far West, this man was elected Judge simply because he was fit for nothing else.

The "boys" did n't want a man above them who knew too much.

When Chipper Charley had been proposed, an old man rose up, turned his hat wrong side out with his fist, twisted his beard around his left hand, spirted a stream of tobacco juice down through an aisle of rugged men and half way across the earthen floor of the Howling Wilderness saloon, and then proceeded to make a speech that killed the candidate dead on the spot.

This was the old man's speech: —

"That won't go down. Too much book larnin."

But the new Judge, or rather the old, bald-headed, dumpy, dirty-faced little fellow, with the dirty shirt and dirty duck breeches, was not a bad man at all. The "boys" had too much hard sense to set up anything but a sort of wooden king to rule over them in this little isolated remote camp and colony of the Sierras. And they were perfectly content with their log too, and never once called out to Jupiter for King Stork.

This old idiotic little Judge, with a round head, round red face, and round belly, had no mind — he had no memory. He had tried everything in the world almost, and always had failed. He had come to never expect anything else. When he rose up to make a speech of thanks to the "boys" for the "unexpected honor," and broke flat down after two or three allusions to the "wonderful climate of Californy," he was perfectly serene, perfectly content. He had got used to breaking down, and it did n't hurt him.

He used to say to his friends in confidence that he certainly would have made a great poet had he begun in his youth. And perhaps he would, for he was certainly fit for nothing else under the sun.

The Forks was the wildest and the freshest bit of the black-white, fir-set, and snow-crowned Sierras that ever the Creator gave, new from His hand, to man.

One thousand men! Not a woman, not a child, down in that cañon of theirs, so deep that the sun never reached them in the Winter and but a little portion of the day in Summer.

Forests, fir and pine, in the cañon, and out of the cañon, up the hills and up the mountains, black and dense, till they broke against the colossal granite peaks far above and crowned in everlasting snow.

Three little streams came tumbling down here from the snow peaks in different directions, meeting with a precision which showed that they knew their ways perfectly through the woods; and from this little union of waters the camp had taken the name of "The Forks."

They had no law, no religion; but, for all that, the men were not bad. It is true they shot and stabbed each other in a rather reckless manner; but then they did it in such a manly sort of a way that but little of the curse of Cain was supposed to follow.

Maybe it was because life was so desolate and dreary that these men threw it away so frequently, and with such refreshing indifference, in the misunderstandings at the Forks; for, after all, they led but wretched lives. That vast freedom of theirs became a sort of desolation.

This was the new Eden. It was so new, it was still damp. You could smell the paint, as it were. Man had just arrived. He had not yet slept. The rib had not yet been taken from his side. He was alone. Behold, these men went up and down the earth, naming new things and possessing them.

Strong, strange men met there from the farthest parts of the world.

Men were grandly honest there. They invariably left gold in their gold-pans from day to day open in the claim — ounces, pounds of it, thousands of dollars to be had for the taking up. Locks and keys were unknown, and, when the miner went down to the Forks on Saturday night to settle his account, he, as a rule, handed the merchant his purse and let him weigh whatever amount he demanded, without question.

When the great Californian novel which has been prophesied of, and for which the literary world seems to be waiting, comes to be written, it will not be a bit popular. And that is because every true Californian, no matter how depraved he may be, somehow has somewhat of the hero and the real man in his make-up. And as for the women that are there, they are angels. So you see there is no one to do the business of the heavy villain.

Sixty miles from the nearest post and neighboring mining camp, it was utterly cut off from communication the biggest half of the year by impassable mountains of snow.

How dark it was down there! The earth it seemed had been cracked open. Then it seemed as if Nature had reached out a hand, smoothed down the ruggedest places, set the whole in a dense and sable forest, topt the mountains round about with everlasting snow, then reached it on to man. And then it looked as if man had come along just as it was nearly ready, slid into the crack, and not being strong enough to get out, resolved to remain there.

The wild beasts were utterly amazed. In

this place even the red man had never yet set his lodge. Deep, and dark, and still. Even the birds were mute. Great snowy clouds, white as the peaks about which they twined, and to which they flew like flocks of birds at night to rest, would droop and droop through the tops of tossing pines, and all the steep and stupendous mountain side on either hand glistened with dew and rain in Summer, or glittered and gleamed in mail and rime of frost and ice in Winter.

These white, foamy, frightened little rivers ran and tumbled together, as if glad to get down the rugged, rocky mountain, and from under the deep and everlasting shadows of fir, and pine, and tamarack, and spruce, and madrona, and the dark sweeping yew, with its beads of scarlet berries. They fairly shouted as they ran and leapt into the open bit of clearing at the Forks. Perhaps they were glad to get away from the grizzlies up there, and were shouting with delight. At all events, they rose together here, united their forces in the friendliest sort of manner, and so moved on down together with a great deal more dignity than before.

You see it was called the Forks simply because it was the Forks. In California things name themselves, or rather Nature names them, and that name is visibly written on the face of things, and every man may understand who can read.

If they call a man Smith in that country it is simply because he looks as if he ought to be called Smith — Smith, and nothing else.

Now there was Limber Tim, one of the first and best men of all the thousand bearded and brawny set of Missourians, a nervous, weakly, sensitive sort of a fellow, who kept always twisting his legs and arms around as he walked, or talked, or tried to sit still, who never could face anything or any one two minutes without flopping over, or turning around, or twisting about, or trying to turn himself wrong side out, and of course anybody instinctively knew his name as soon as he saw him.

The baptismal name of Limber Tim was Thomas Adolphus Grosvenor. And yet these hairy, half-savage, unread Missourians, who had stopped here in their great pilgrimage of the plains, and never yet seen a city, or the sea, or a school-house, or a church, knew perfectly well that there was a mistake in this matter the moment they saw him, and that his name was Limber Tim.

It is pretty safe to say that if one of these wild and unread Missourians had met this timid limber man meandering down the mountain trail — met him, I mean, for the first time in all his life, without ever having heard of him before — he would have gone straight up to him, taken him by the hand, and shaking it heartily, said,

"How d'ye do, Limber Tim?"

The Forks had just been "struck." Some Missourians had slid into this crack in the earth, had found the little streams full of gold, and making sure that they had not been followed, and, like Indians, obliterating all signs of their trail, they went out slily as they came, struck the great stream of immigrants from the plains, and turned the current of their friends from Pike into this crack of the earth till it flowed full, and there was room for no more. The Forks was at once a little Republic; a sort of San Marino without a patron saint or a single tower.

A thousand men, I said, and not a single woman; that is, not one woman who was what these men called "on the square." Of course, two or three fallen women, soiled doves, had followed the fortunes of these hardy fellows into the new camp, but they were in some respects worse than no women at all.

As was usual with these fallen angels, they kept the camp, or certain elements in the camp, in a constant state of uproar, and contributed more to the rapid filling-up of the new grave-yard up on the hill than all other causes put together. The fat and dirty little judge, who really wanted to keep peace, and who felt that he must always give an opinion, when asked why it was that the boys would fight so dreadfully over these women, and kill each other, said, "It is all owing to this glorious climate of Californy."

The truth is, they fought and killed each other, and kept up the regular Sunday funeral all Summer through, not because these bad women were there, but because the good women were not there. Yet possibly "the glorious climate of Californy" had a bit to do with the hot blood of the men, after all.

CHAPTER II.

LITTLE BILLIE PIPER.

NOBODY knew when he came. Perhaps nobody cared. He was the smallest man in the camp. In fact he was not a man. He was only a boyish, girlish-looking creature that came and went at will. He was so small he crowded no one, and so no one cried out about him, or paid him any attention, so long as they were all busily taking possession of and measuring off the new Eden.

What a shy, sensitive, girlish-looking man! His boyish face was beautiful, dreamy and childish. It was sometimes half-hidden in a cloud of yellow hair that fell down about it, and was always being pushed back by a small white hand, that looked helpless enough, in the battle of life among these bearded and brawny men on the edge of the new world.

He had a little bit of a cabin on the hillside, not far way from the Forks, and lived alone. This living alone was always rated to be a bad sign. It was counted selfish. Few men lived alone in the mines. In fact the cabins in the mines were generally jammed and crowded as tight with men as if they had been little tin boxes packed with sardines.

When the bees in this new and busy hive began to settle down to their work; when they in fact got a little of the hurry and flurry of their own affairs a little off their minds, and they had a bit of time to look into the affairs of others, they began to reflect that no man had ever entered this little cabin.

Cabins in the mines in those days were generally open to all. "The latch string," to use the expression of the Sierras, hung on the outside to strangers. But this one peculiar cabin had no "latch-string" for any man.

Men began to get curious. I assert that curiosity is not the monopoly of sex. One Sunday some half idle and wholly inquisitive men went up to this cabin as they passed in the trail, which ran hard by, and asked for a drink of water.

A little hand brought a dipper of water to the door. A boy face lifted up timidly to the great bearded men from Missouri as they in turn drank and passed the big tin dipper from one to the other till it was drained; then the little hand took the dipper back again and disappeared, while the men, half ashamed and wholly confounded, stumbled on up the trail.

The boy had been so civil, so shy, so modest, and yet, when occasion offered, so kind withal, that few could refuse to be his friends; and now he had, only by lifting his eyes, won over this knot of half-vulgar, half-ruffianly fellows wholly to his side.

Once the saloon-keeper, the cinnamon-haired man of the Howling Wilderness, as the one whisky shop of this New Eden was called, met him on the trail as he was going out with a pick and shovel on his shoulder, to prospect for gold.

"What is your name, my boy?"

"Billie Piper."

The timid brown eyes looked up through the cluster of yellow curls, as the boy stepped aside to let the big man pass; and the two, without other words, went on their ways.

Oddly enough they allowed this boy to keep his name. They called him Little Billie Piper.

He was an enigma to the miners. Sometimes he looked to be only fifteen. Then again he was very thoughtful. The fair brow was wrinkled sometimes; there were lines, sabre cuts of time, on the fair delicate face, and then he looked to be at least double that age.

He worked, or at least he went out to work, every day with his pick and pan and shovel; but almost always they saw him standing by the running stream, looking into the water, dreaming, seeing in Nature's mirror the snowy clouds that blew in moving mosaic overhead and through and over the tops of the tossing firs.

He rarely spoke to the men more than in monosyllables. Yet when he did speak to them his language was so refined, so far above their common speech, and his voice was so soft, and his manner so gentle that they saw in him, in some sort, a superior.

Yet Limber Tim, the boy-man, came pretty near to this boy's life. At least he stood nearer to his heart than any one. Their lives were nearer the same level. One Sunday they stood together on the hill by the grave-yard above the Forks.

"Tell me," said the boy, laying his hand on the arm of his companion, and looking earnestly and sadly in his face, "Tell me, Tim, why it is that they always have the grave-yard on a hill. Is it because it is a little nearer to heaven?"

His companion did not understand. And yet he did understand, and was silent.

They sat down together by and by and looked up out of the great cañon at the drifting white clouds, and the boy said, looking into heaven, as if to himself,

"O! fleets of clouds that flee before
The burly winds of upper seas."

Then as the sudden twilight fell and they went down the hill together, the white crooked moon, as if it had just been broken from off the snow peak that it had been hiding behind, came out with a star.

"How the red star hangs to the moon's white horn."

There was no answer, for his companion was awed to utter silence.

One day, Bunker Hill, a humped-back and unhappy woman of uncertain ways, passed through the crowd in the Forks. Some of the rough men laughed and made remarks. This boy was there also. Lifting his eyes to one of these men at his side, he said:

"God has made some women a little plain, in order that he might have some women that are wholly good."

These things began to be noised about. All things have their culmination. Even the epizootic has one worst day. Things only go so far. Rockets only rise so high, then they explode, and all is dark and still.

The Judge stood straddled out before the roaring fire of the Howling Wilderness one night, tilting up the tails of his coat with his two hands which he had turned in behind him, as he stood there warming the upper ends of his short legs, and listening to these questions and the comments of the men. At last, he seemed to have an inspiration, and tilting forward on his toes, and bringing his head very low down, and his coat-tails very high up, he said, solemnly:

"Fellow-citizens, it 's a poet."

Then bringing out his right hand, and reaching it high in the air, as he poised on his right leg:

"In this glorious climate of Californy—"

"Be gad, it is!" cried an Irishman, jumping up, "a Bryan! A poet, a rale, live, Lord O'Bryan."

And so the status of the strange boy was fixed at the Forks. He was declared to be a poet, and was no more a wonder. Curiosity was satisfied.

"It is something to know that it is no worse," growled a very practical old man, as he held a pipe in his teeth and rubbed his tobacco between his palms.

He spoke of it as if it had been a case of the small-pox, and as if he was thinking how to best prevent the spread of the infection.

CHAPTER III.

THE FIRST WOMAN IN THE FORKS.

ONE day Limber Tim came up from the Howling Wilderness, all excitement: all gyrations, and gimlets, and corkscrews. He twisted himself around a sapling — this great, overgrown, six-foot boy without a beard — and shouting down to his "pardner" in the mine, Old Sandy, who stood at the bottom of the open claim, leaning on his pick, resting a moment, looking into the bright bubbling water that burst laughing from the bank before him, dreaming a bit in the freshness about him; and said, "Hallo! I say! a widder's come to town. D 'ye hear? A widder; one what 's up and up, and on the square."

Sandy only looked up, for he was getting old, and gray, and wrinkled. Then he looked at the silver stream that ran from the bank and through the rocks at his feet, and called to him in the pleasant, balmy sunset, sweet with the smell of fir, and he did not disturb the water again with his pick. It looked too pretty, laughed, and sparkled, and leapt, and made him glad and yet sad.

A poet was this man Sandy, a painter, a sculptor, a mighty moralist; a man who could not write his name.

He laid down his pick, for the sun was just pitching his last lances at the snow-peaks away up yonder above the firs, above the clouds, and night was coming down with steady steps to possess this chasm in the earth.

Limber Tim untwisted himself from the sapling as Sandy came up from the mine, twisting his great shaggy beard with his right hand, while he carried his black slouch hat in his left, and the two sauntered on toward their cabin together, while Sandy's great gum boots whetted together as he walked.

The "Parson" was in a neighboring cabin when it was announced that the first woman had come to the camp. The intelligence was received in a profound silence.

There was a piece of looking-glass tacked up over the fire-place of this cabin.

Old Baldy whistled a little air, and walked up to this glass, sidewise, silently, and stood there smoothing down his beard.

"Ginger blue!" cried the Parson, at last, bounding up from his bench, and throwing out his arms, as if throwing the words from the ends of his fingers. "Ginger blue! hell-ter-flicker!" And here he danced around the cabin in a terrible state of excitement, to the tune of a string of iron-clad oaths that fell like chain-shot. They called him the Parson, because it was said he could outswear any man in the camp, and that was saying a great deal, wonderful as were his achievements in this line.

After the announcement, every one of the ten men there took a look at the little triangular fragment of looking-glass that was tacked up over the fire-place.

The arrival of Eve in Paradise was certainly an event; but she came too early in the world's history to create much sensation.

Stop here, and fancy the arrival of the first woman on earth to-day — in this day of committees, conventions, brass-band receptions, and woman's rights!

You imagine a princess had come to camp, a good angel, with song and harps, or, at the least, carpet-bags, and extended crinoline, waterfalls, and false hair, a pack-train of Saratoga trunks, and all the adjuncts of civilization. Not at all. She had secured a cabin, by some accident, very near to that of the boy poet, and settled down there quietly to go to work.

Yes, Limber Tim had "seed" her. She had ridden the bell mule of the pack-train down the mountain and into town. He told how the hats went up in the air from in and about the Howling Wilderness, and how the boys had gone up in rows to the broken looking-glass in the new barber-shop, and how some had even polished their bowie-knives on their boots, and sat down and tried to see themselves in the shining blade, and adjust their dress accordingly.

In a little time Sandy bent silently over the table in the cabin, and with his sleeves rolled up high on his great hairy arms, and kneaded away at the dough in the gold pan in silence, while Limber Tim wrestled nervously with the frying-pan by the fire.

"Is she purty, Limber?"

"Purty, Sandy? She 's purtier nur a spotted dog."

Sandy sighed, for he felt that there was little hope for him, and again fell into a moody silence.

There was a run that night on the little Jew shop at the corner of the Howling Wilderness. Before midnight the little kinky-headed Israelite had not a shirt, collar, or handkerchief, or white fabric of any kind whatever in the shop.

It might have been a bit of first-class and old-fashioned chivalry that had lain dormant in these great hairy breasts, or it might have been their strict regard for the appropriateness of names that made these men at once call her the "Widder;" or it might have been some sudden revelation, a sort of inspiration, given to the first man who saw her as she rode down the mountain into camp, or the first man who spoke of her as she rode blushing through their midst with her pretty face held modestly down; but be all that as it may, certainly there was no design, no delay, no hesitation about it from the first. And yet the appellation was singularly appropriate, and perhaps suggested to this poor, lone little woman, daring to cross the mountains, and to come down into this great chasm of the earth, among utter strangers, the conduct of her life.

The first woman came unheralded. Like all good things on earth, she came quietly as a snowflake down in their midst, without ado or demonstration.

Who she was or where she came from no one seemed to know. Perhaps the propriety of questioning occurred to some of the men of the camp, but it never found expression. I had rather say, however, that when they found there was a real live woman in camp, a decent woman, who was willing to work and take her place beside the men in the great battle — bear her part in the common curse which demands that we shall toil to eat, they quietly accepted the fact, as men do the fact of the baby's arrival, without any question whatever.

This was not really the first woman to come into the camp of this thousand of bearded men; and yet it was the first. There were now five or six, maybe more, down at the Forks — some from Sydney, some from New Orleans — waifs of the foam, painted children of passion.

I am not disposed to put all these women in the catalogue of saints. They were very devils, some of them.

These women set man against man, and that Winter made many a crimson place in the great snow banks in the streets. They started the first graveyard at the Forks; and kept it recruited too, every holiday, and almost every Sunday.

True, they did some good. I do not deny that. For example, I have in my mind now the picture of one, Bunker Hill, holding the head of a brave young fellow, shot through the temple, his long black hair in strings and streaming with blood. She held him so till he died; and mourned and would not be separated from him while a hope or a breath remained — the blood on her hands, on her face, all over her costly silks and lace, and on the floor.

Then she had him buried elegantly as possible; sent for a preacher away over to Yreka to say the funeral service; put evergreens about his grave, and refused to be comforted.

All this was very beautiful — a touch of tenderness in it all; but it was spoiled by the reflection that she had allured and almost forced the fellow into the fight, in hopes of revenging herself on the man whom she hated, and by whose hand he had to fall.

There was another woman there who was very benevolent — in fact, they all were liberal with their money, and were the first and freest to bestow upon the needy. This woman was a Mexican — from Durango, I think; and her name was Dolores. Gentle in her manner, patient, sad; not often in the difficulties that distinguished the others; but generally alone, and by far the best liked of all these poor Magdalens. This good nature of hers made her most accessible, and so she was most sought for deeds of charity. Toward Spring it was said she was ill; but no one seemed to know, or maybe no one cared.

If you will stop here to consider, it will occur to you that it is a man's disposition to avoid a sick woman; but a woman's disposition to seek out a sick man and nurse him back to health. This being true, here is a text for the Sorosis.

A bank had caved on a man — only a prospecter, a German, who lived away in a little cabin on the hillside — and crushed him frightfully. The man was penniless and alone, and help had to come from the camp.

Some one went to Dolores. She was in her room or cabin, out a little way from any one, alone and ill, sitting up in bed, looking "wild enough," as the man afterwards stated. He told her what had happened. She leaned her head on her hand a moment, and then lifted it, looked up, and drew a costly ring from her finger, the only one on her pale, thin hand, and gave it to the man, who hurried away to get other aid elsewhere.

Now there was nothing very odd or unusual in a woman giving a ring. That was often done. In fact, there was scarcely any coin on the Creek. In cases of this kind a man generally gave the biggest nugget or specimen he had in his pocket, a ring if he could not do better, sometimes a six-shooter, and so on, and let them make the best of it, but always something, if that something was possible. Let this be said and remembered of these brave old men of the mountains.

A few days after this, it came out that Dolores was dead. Then it was whispered that she had starved to death. This last was said with a sort of a shudder. It came out with a struggle between the teeth, as if the men were afraid to say it.

On investigation, it was found that the poor woman had been ill some time, had lost her bloom and freshness; and what becomes of a woman of this kind, who has no money, when she has lost her bloom and strength? never had much money, always gave it away to the needy as fast as she got it, and so had nothing to fight the world with when she fell ill.

Then the man with the rent, the lord of the log cabin — a cross between a Shylock-Jew and a flint-faced Yankee — took her rings and jewels, one by one. The baker grew exacting, and finally the butcher refused to bring her meat. And that was all there was of it. That was the end.

That butcher never succeeded there after that. Some one wrote "Small Pox" over his shop every night for a month, and it was shunned like a pest-house. But all that did not bring poor Dolores back to life. The ring was an antique gold, with a costly stone, and a Spanish name, which showed her to have been of good family. A wedding ring.

But this woman, however, was an exception, and at best, when in health, save her generous and sympathetic nature, was probably no angel.

One of these meddlesome men, a hungry,

lean, unsatisfied fellow; a man with a nose sharp and inquisitive enough to open a cast-iron cannon ball, said one night to a knot of men at the Howling Wilderness saloon:

"Why widder? why call her the widder? who knows that she was ever married at all?"

A man silently and slowly arose at this, and firmly doubled up his fist. He stood there towering above that fellow, and looking down upon that sharp inquisitive nose as if he wanted to drive it back into the middle of his head.

"But maybe she's a maid," answered the terrified nose in haste and fear.

The other sat down, slowly and silently, as he had risen, and perfectly satisfied that no insult had been intended. This was Sandy.

The Judge was there, and as the conversation had fallen through by this man's remark, he felt called upon to resume it in a friendly sort of a way, and said:

"No, no, she's not a maid, I reckon, not an old maid." He scratched his bald head above his ear and went on, for the big man at his side began to double up his knuckles. "I should say she's a widder. You see, the maids never gits this far. They seem to spile first."

The Judge spoke as if talking of a sort of pickled oyster or smoked ham.

CHAPTER IV.

SUNDAY IN THE SIERRAS.

NEVER did the press feed on a political war, or a calumniated poet, as these men of the Howling Wilderness fed on this one woman of the Forks.

Yet let it be remembered they always, and to a man, with scarce an exception, spoke of her with the profoundest respect. Few of them had had the pleasure of seeing her, fewer still of speaking to her, yet she was the ever-present topic. Even the weather in a London Winter is hardly more popular a theme, than was the Widow when they met in knots in the little town after the day's work was over.

The brave, silent, modest little woman had put her hands to the plow at once. These men knew perfectly well that honest people had no business there but to work; and when her little hands, that did not look at all as if they had been used to toil, took hold of the hard fact of life, and the little face bent above the wash-tub, and the fine white brow glistened with a diadem of diamonds that grew there as a price for bread, they loved her to a man.

What strange savage scenes were enacted here before the arrival of this one good woman. Every Saturday night was a sort of carnival of death. Men went about from drinking-shop to drinking-shop, howling like Modocs, swinging their pistols, proclaiming themselves chiefs, and seeking for bloody combat. They gave the country a name and a reputation in this first year of gold mining in the Sierras that will survive them every one.

On Sunday the scene was somewhat changed. With all their savagery and wildness and nonsense, it was always understood that the work of the week must go on, and Sunday was the great day of preparation.

Sunday was not a day of rest. It is true the miners slept a little later on Sunday morning, but Sunday was to all a day of terror and petty troubles beyond measure. It always came to some one's turn, every Sunday morning, in every mess or cabin, to begin his week's cooking for his mess, and for that reason, if for no other, there was at least one man miserable in every cabin whenever the dreaded Sunday came.

Then there was the mending of clothes! Mercy! Great big hairy men sitting up and out on the hillside with their backs up against the pines, sitting there out of sight, half naked, stitching, stitching, stitching, and swearing at every stitch.

But the great and terrible event of Sunday, before the Widow came, was the washing of clothes. Neither love nor money could induce any one save the uncertain little Chinaman to undertake this task for them, before the arrival of the Widow. Therefore when Sunday came these men went down in line, silently and solemnly, to the little mountain stream (allowed to rest and run clear and crystal-like on Sunday), and stood in a row along its banks, in top-boots, duck breeches, red shirts, and great broad hats. Then, at a word, each man laid aside his hat, undid the bosom of his shirt, straightened his arms, and drew his shirt up and over his head, and then fastened his belt, and squatted by the stream, and rubbed and rubbed and rubbed. Brawny-muscled men, nude above the waist, "naked and not ashamed," hairy-breasted and bearded, noble, kingly men — miners washing their shirts in a mountain-stream of the Sierras. Thoughtful, earnest, splendid men! Boughs above them, pine-tops toying with the sun that here and there reached through like fingers pointing at them from the far, pure purple of the sky.

And a stillness so profound, perfect, holy as a temple! Nature knows her Sabbath.

I would give more for a painting of this scene — that sun, that sky and wood, the water there, the brave, strong men, the thinkers and the workers there, nude and natural, silent and sincere, bending to their work — than for all the battle scenes that could be hung upon a palace wall. When the great man comes, the painter of the true and great, these men will be remembered.

It is said that Diogenes, when he saw a boy drinking water from his hand, scooped up from the stream, threw away his cup, the last utensil he had retained.

This shirt-washing went on in some camps for years. These men were compelled to study simplicity, and did from necessity nearly what the cynic did from caprice. Where every man had to carry his effects on his back for days and days, through steep and rugged paths, an extra garment was not to be thought of. Men got used to the one-shirt system, and seemed to like it. Some stuck to it with a tenacity hardly respectful to the near approach of civilization.

Once upon a time, to coin a new beginning, a younger brother came out to visit one of these brave old miners, now gray and grizzled, but true to his old traditions and habits of life. He called on him on Sunday, entered his cabin, and found him covered in his blankets.

"What, my brother, are you sick?" said he, after the first salutations and embraces were exchanged.

"Sick! No, not sick."

"Then why are you in bed?"

"Oh! I washed my shirt to-day and got in bed to let it dry."

"Why! Have n't you got but the one shirt?"

"But the one shirt! No! Do you think a man wants a *thousand* shirts?"

These men were mostly shy with their letters and their tales of love. That was sacred ground, upon which no strange, rude feet could pass. No gold-hunter there, perhaps, but had his love — his one only love, without a chance or possibility of changing the object of his devotion, even if he had desired it. Men must love as well as women. It is the most natural and, consequently, the most proper thing on earth. Imagine how intensified and how tender a man's devotion would become under circumstances like these. The one image in his heart, the one hope — HER. So much time to think, bending to the work in the running water under the trees, on the narrow trail beneath the shadows of the forest, by the camp and cabin-fire, her face and hers only, with no new face rising up, crossing his path, confronting him for days, for months, for years — see how holy a thing his love would grow to be. This, you observe, is a new man, a new manner of lover. Love, I say, is a requirement, a necessity. It is as necessary for a complete man to love as it is for him to breathe pure air. And it is as natural.

These men, being so far removed from any personal contact with the objects of their affections, and only now and then at long intervals receiving letters, all marked and re-marked across the backs from the remailings from camp to camp, of course knew of no interruptions in the current of their devotion, and loved in a singularly earnest and sincere way. I doubt if there be anything like it in history.

When men go to war, they have the glory and excitement of battle to allure them, then the eyes of many women are upon them; they are not locked up like these men of the Sierras, with only their work and the one thing to think of. When they go to sea, sailors find new faces in every port; but these men, from the time they crossed the Missouri or left the Atlantic coast, had known no strange gods, hardly heard a woman's voice, till they returned.

But let us return to this one firm first woman, who had come into camp and taken at once upon her shoulders the task of washing and mending the miners' clothes.

Men, even the most bloated and besotted, walked as straight as possible up the trail that led by the Widow's cabin, as they passed that way at night; and kept back their jokes and war-whoops till far up the creek and out of her hearing in the pines.

A general improvement was noticed in all who dwelt in sight or hearing of her cabin. In fact, that portion of the creek became a sort of West End, and cabin rent went up in that vicinity. Men were made better, gentler. No doubt of that. If, then, one plain woman, rude herself by nature, can do so much, what is not left for gentle and cultured woman, who is or should be the true missionary of the West — the world?

A woman's weakness is her strength,

She was tall, gentle, genial too, and soon a favorite with her many, many patrons. She had a scar on the left side of her face, they said, reaching from the chin to the cheek; but with a woman's tact, she always kept her right side to her company, and the scar was not always noticed.

What had been her history, what troubles she had had, what tempests she had stood against, or what great storm had blown this solitary woman far into the great black sea of firs that belts about and lies in the shadow of the Sierras, like a lone white sea-dove you sometimes find far out in the China seas, no man knew; and, be it said to the credit of the Forks, no man cared to inquire.

This meeting together, this coming and going of thousands of men from all parts of the earth, where each man stood on the character he made there in a day, deadened curiosity, perhaps.

At all events, you can go, a stranger, to-day, any where along the Pacific, and, if your character indicates the gentleman, you are accepted as such, and no man cares to ask of your antecedents. A convenient thing, I grant, for many; but, nevertheless, a good thing, and a correct thing for any country.

The old Jewish law of every seven years forgiving each man his debt was an age in advance of our laws of to-day; and, if any means could be devised by which every seven years to forgive all men their offences, and let them begin life anew all together, an even start, it would be better still.

How the work did pour in upon this first woman in this wild Eden set with thorns and with thistles! There were not many clothes in the Forks that were worth washing, but the few pieces that were presentable came almost every day to the door of the Widow to be taken in by the little hand that ever opened to the knock of the miners' knuckles on the door, and reached through the partly opened place, and drew back timidly and with scarce a word.

No man had yet entered her cabin. The wise little woman! If one man had been so favored, without good and sufficient reason, then jealousy, unless others had been allowed to enter also, would have made a funeral, and very soon, too, with that one favored man the central figure.

No man had entered that cabin; but a boy had, and oftentime too. In fact from the first little Billie Piper, whose cabin, as I have said, stood hard by, seemed to be as much at home and as much in place with the Widow as he was out of place with the men. The friendship here made him enemies elsewhere. Such is human nature.

CHAPTER V.

WASHEE – WASHEE.

TWO days after the Widow had arrived, Washee-Washee, as the "boys" had named him, stood out on the steps of his cabin all the afternoon, looking up the Forks and down the Forks, and wondering what in the world was the reason the "boys" did not come creaking along and screeching their great gum boots together, with their extra shirt for wash wadded down in one of the spacious legs.

Three days after the Widow had arrived she had absorbed all the business. Four days after she had arrived, she absorbed Washee-Washee. And now it was the brown hand of little moon-eyed Washee-Washee that reached through the door, took the clothes, and handed them out again, or at least such portions as he chose to hand out, to the bearded giants standing there, patiently waiting at the door of the Widow's cabin.

The face of the Widow was now almost entirely invisible. It was as if there was no sun at the Forks, and all the sky was in a perpetual eclipse of clouds.

Soon there was trouble. Clothes began to disappear. One bearded sovereign, a gallant man, who refused to complain because there was a woman in the case, was observed to wear his coat buttoned very closely up to his chin; and that too in midday in Summer. This good man had at first lost only his extra shirt. He did not complain. He simply went to bed on Sunday, sent his shirt early to the wash, expecting to rise in the afternoon, "dress," and go to town. A week went by. The man could not stay in bed till the day of judgment, so he rose up, buttoned up to the throat, and went down to buy another supply.

Other circumstances, not dissimilar in result, began to be talked of quietly; and men began to question whether or not after all the camp had been greatly the gainer by this new element in its population.

One afternoon there was a commotion at the door of the Widow's cabin. Sandy was in trouble with Washee-Washee. The moon-eyed little man tried to get back into the house, but the great big giant had been too long a patient and uncomplaining sufferer to let him escape now, and he reached for his queue, and drew him forth as a showman does a black snake from a cage.

The Widow saw the great hairy face of this grizzly giant, and retreated far back into the cabin. She was certain she was terribly afraid of this great big awkward half-clad exasperated man, and therefore, with a woman's consistency, she came to the door, and in a voice softer than running water to Sandy's ears, asked what could be the matter?

Sandy was taken by surprise, and could not say a word. He only rolled his great head from one shoulder to the other, got his hands lashed up somehow in his leather belt, and stood there sadly embarrassed.

But who ever saw an embarrassed Chinaman? The innocent little fellow, turning his soft brown almond eyes up to the Widow, told her, as poor Sandy stared on straight down the hill, that this dreadful "Amelikan" wanted him to leave her, and to go home with him, to be his wife.

When Sandy heard this last he disappeared, crestfallen and utterly crushed. He went home; but not to rest. He told Limber Tim all about what had happened. How he had stood it all in silence, till it came to the last shirt. How the Chinaman had lied, and how he was now certain that it was this same little celestial who had been robbing him. Limber Tim raised himself on his elbow where he lay in his bunk, and looking at Sandy, struck out emphatically with his hand, and cried —

"Lay fur him!"

Sandy drew on his great gum boots again. Limber Tim rose up, and then the two men kept creaking, and screeching and whetting their great boots together, as they went, without speaking, and in single file down the hill towards town.

There was an expression of ineffable peace and tranquility on the face of Washee-Washee that twilight, as he wended his way from the Widow's cabin to his own. His day's work was done; and the little man's face looked the soul of repose. Possibly he was saying with the great good poet, whose lines you hear at evening time, on the lips of nearly every English artisan —

> "Something attempted, something done,
> Has earn'd a night's repose."

Washee-Washee looked strangely fat for a Chinaman, as he peacefully toddled down the trail, still wearing, as he neared his cabin, that look of calm delight and perfect innocence, such only as the pure in heart are supposed to wear. His hands were drawn up and folded calmly across his obtruding stomach, as if he feared he might possibly burst open, and wanted to be ready to hold himself together.

In the great-little republic there, where all had begun an even and equal race in the battle of life, where all had begun as beggars, this tawny little man from the far-off Flowery Kingdom was alone; he was the only representative of his innumerable millions in all that camp. And he did seem so fat, so perfectly full of satisfaction. Perhaps he smiled to think how fat he was, and, too, how he had flourished in the little democracy.

He was making a short turn in the trail, still holding his clasped hands over his extended stomach, still smiling peacefully out of his half-shut eyes:

"Washee! Washee!"

A double bolt of thunder was in his ears. A tremendous hand reached out from behind a pine, and then the fat little Chinaman squatted down and began to wilt and melt beneath it.

"Washee-Washee, come!"

Washee-Washee was not at all willing to come; but that made not the slightest difference in the world to Sandy. The little almond-eyed man was not at all heavy. Old flannel shirts, cotton overalls, stockings, cotton collars and cambric handkerchiefs never are heavy, no matter how well they may be wadded in, and padded away, and tucked up, and twisted under an outer garment; and so before he had time to say a word he was on his way to the Widow's with Sandy, while Limber Tim, with his mouth half-open, came corkscrewing up the trail, and grinding and whetting his screechy gum boots together after them.

There is a fine marble statue in the garden at Naples, near the massive marble head of Virgil, which represents some great giant as striding along with some little pigmy thrown over his shoulder, which he is carelessly holding on by the heel. Sandy looked not wholly unlike that statue, as he strode up the trail with Washee-Washee.

He reached the door of the Widow's cabin, knocked with the knuckles of his left hand, while his right hand held on to an ankle that hung down over his left shoulder, and calmly waited an answer.

The door half-way opened.

"Beg pardon, mum."

He bowed stiffly as he said this, and then shifting Washee-Washee round, quietly took his other heel in his other hand, and proceeded to shake him up and down, and dance him and stand him gently on his head, until the clothes began to burst out from under his blue seamless garment, and to peep through his pockets, and to reach down around his throat and dangle about his face, till the little man was nearly smothered.

Then Sandy set him down a moment to rest, and he looked in his face as he sat there, and it had the same peaceful smile, the same calm satisfaction as before. The little man now put his head to one side, shut his pretty brown eyes a little tighter at the corners, and opened his mouth the least bit in the world, and put out his tongue as if he was about to sing a hymn.

Then Sandy took him up again. He smiled again sweeter than before. Sandy tilted him sidewise, and shook him again. Then there fell a spoon, then a pepper-box, and then a small brass candlestick ; and at last, as he rolled him over and shook the other side, there came out a machine strangely and wonderfully made of whalebone and brass, and hooks and eyes, that Sandy had never seen before, and did not at all understand, but supposed was either a fish trap or some new invention for washing gold.

Then Limber Tim, who had screwed his back up against the palings, and watched all this with his mouth open, came down, and reaching out with his thumb and finger, as if they had been a pair of tongs, took the garments one by one, named them, for he knew them and their owners well, and laid them silently aside. Then he took Washee-Washee from the hands of Sandy and stood him up, or tried to stand him up alone. He looked like a flagstaff with the banner falling loosely around it in an indolent wind. He held him up by the queue awhile, but he wilted and sank down gently at his feet, all the time smiling sweetly as before, all the time looking up with a half-closed eye and half-parted lips, as though he was enjoying himself perfectly, and would like to laugh, only that he had too much respect for the present company.

"If I could only shake the lies out of him, mum, as easily as I did this 'ere spoon, and this 'ere candlestick, and this 'ere, this 'ere" — Sandy had stooped and picked up the articles as he spoke, and now was handing them to the Widow in triumph.

"Poor little, helpless, pitiful fellow!"

The Widow was looking straight at the celestial, who sat there piled up in a little bit of a heap, the limpest thing in all the Forks perhaps, save Limber Tim.

"Let him go, please; let him go. Bring the things and come in. You can go now, John; but do n't do so any more. It is not right."

The Widow smiled in pity as she said this to Washee-Washee. The Chinaman understood the first proposition perfectly, but not the last at all. To him all this was simply a bad investment. To him it was only a little shipwreck;

and having been taught by the philosophers of his country to prepare for adversity in the hour of prosperity, he was not at all lacking in resignation now. He rose up, smiled that patient and peaceful smile of his, and wended his way to his home.

Sandy looked a moment at the retreating hungry-looking little Chinaman, and then thrust his two great hands into his two great pockets, and tilting his head, first on the left shoulder and then on the right, tried hard to look the Widow in the face, but found himself contemplating the toes of his great gum boots.

"Will you not come in?"

The man rolled forward. He sat down in the Widow's cabin in a perfect glow of excitement and delight.

I am bound to admit that, upright and great as Sandy was, he kept thinking to himself, "What will the Judge and the boys say of this?" He even was glad in his heart that Limber Tim stood with his back glued up against the palings on the outside, and his hands reached back and wound in and around the rails, so that he could testify to the boys, tell it, in fact, to the world, that he had entered in, and sat down in the Widow's cabin.

It was not easy work for Sandy sitting there. He soon began to suffer. He hitched about and twisted around on the broad wooden stool as if he had sat down on a very hot stove.

The Widow sat a little way back across the cabin, a bit of work in her lap, looking up at Sandy now, and now dropping her half-sad blue eyes down to her work, and all the time, in a low sweet way, doing every word of the talking.

Sandy's hot stove kept getting hotter and hotter. He began to wish he was down with the boys at the Howling Wilderness, consulting the oracle of cocktails. All at once he seemed to discover his great long legs. They seemed to him as if they reached almost clean across the cabin, like two great anacondas going to swallow up the Widow. He fished them up, curved them, threw his two great hands across them, nursed them affectionately, but they seemed more in the way and uglier than ever before. Then he thrust them out again, but jerked them back instantly, and drove them back under his bench as if they had been two big and unruly bull-dogs, and he nearly upset himself in doing it. They had fairly frightened him, they were surely never half so long before. It seemed to him as if they would reach across the room, through the wall, and even down to the Howling Wilderness. He twisted them up under the bench and got them fast there, and was glad of it, for now they would not and could not run out and rush across the room at the Widow.

But now poor Sandy saw another skeleton. His eyes came upon them suddenly, in a sort of discovery. It seemed as if he had just found them out for the first time, and knew them for mortal enemies, and determined to do away with them at once, and at any sacrifice.

Such hands! had the Widow really been looking at them all this time? the back of that hand was big and rough as the bark of a tree. That finger nail had a white rim of dough around it; that thumb nail was as big and about as dirty as a crevicing spoon! He picked up that hand, thrust it under him, sat firmly over on that side, and held it down and out of sight with all his might. The other one lay there, still in the way. It was uglier than the one he had just slain and hidden away in the bush.

There was dirt enough about the nails to make a small mining claim. He rolled the hand over and over on his lap, as if it had been somebody's baby; and a baby with the colic. At last, in a state of desperation, he rolled it off and let it fall and take care of itself. It hung down at his side like a great big felon from the scaffold.

It twisted and swung around there as if it had just been hung up by the neck in the expiation of some awful crime. It felt to Sandy as if it weighed a ton. He tried to lift it up again, to take care of it, to nurse it, to turn it over on its stomach, to stroke it, and talk to it, and pity it, and soothe away its colic, but lo! he could not lift it. He began to perspire, he was so very warm. It was the warmest time that Sandy had ever seen. All this time Sandy had sat close by the door, and not one word had he uttered.

The Widow rose up, laid her work on the table, all the time smiling sweetly, half sadly, and going up to the fire-place, took from the box in the corner, pine knot after pine knot, and laid them on the blazing fire.

"Come, the evening is chilly, will you not sit closer to the fire?"

Sandy sat still as the statue of Moses in the Vatican, but that abominable felon hanging by the neck at his side kept twisting around and around and around as if he never would die or be still. The Widow sat down with her work as before, and this time she began to talk about the weather, trusting that on this subject at least, her great good friend could open his lips and speak.

"How very cold it is this evening. The chill of the snow is in the air; it blows down from the banks of snow on the mountain, and

I fancy it may be cold here in this rickety cabin the Summer through."

Still the ugly convict, that now began to grow black in the face, swung and twisted at his side; but he did not speak.

"Do you not feel cold?"

"Yes 'um."

The two words came out like the bark of a bull-dog; as if one of the brutes he had drawn back under his bench had stuck out his nose and yelped in the face of the Widow, and Sandy was frightened nearly to death. The perspiration dropped from his brow to his hand, and he knew that things could not last in this way much longer. The bull-dogs would be out, and he knew it. The dead man that he was sitting down upon would rise up to judgment, and the felon at his side was only swinging and turning and twisting more than before.

Sandy shut his eyes and attempted to rise. His gum boots screeched, the bench creaked as he began to undouble himself. It turned up and hung on behind him as if it had been a lobster. He shook it off, and began to tower up like a pine. He feared he would pierce through the roof, and began to look out through the half-open door, and to stretch out the prostrate hand. Then he stood still and was more bewildered than before. The Widow was looking straight at him, and expecting him to speak. He wished he had not got up at all. If he was only back on that overthrown bench, with the dead man beneath him, and the bull-dogs below, and the felon swinging loosely at his side, how happy he would be. He tried to speak, tried like a man, but if it had been to save his life, to save her life, the world, he could not find will to shape one word. He backed and blundered and stumbled across the threshold and drew a breath, such a breath! the first he had drawn for half an hour, as he stood outside, with the Widow's little feet following to the threshold, and her pretty miniature face looking up to his as if looking up to the top of a pine.

"You will come again, will you not? you have been so very kind; please to call, step in as you pass, and rest. It is so lonesome here, you know! nobody that anybody knows. And then you are such good company."

And then the pretty little Widow with the sad sweet face, laughed the prettiest little laugh that ever was laughed this side that other Eden with its one fair woman.

Limber Tim closed his mouth and unscrewed himself from the palings on the fence without as Sandy appeared, and the two took their way to their cabin.

"And you are such good company." That was all Sandy could remember. What could he have said? He tried and tried to recall his observations, whatever they may have been, on the various topics of the day, but in vain. He could only remember the circumstance of driving two ugly bull-dogs back under his bench, of slaying and hiding away his mortal enemy, and then hanging a felon for high treason; and then chiefest of all, "You will come again, it is lonesome here; you are such good company."

"You are such good company." The wind sang it through the trees as he wended his way home. The water, away down in the cañon below the trail, sang it soft and low and sweet, sang it ever, and nothing more, and the teakettle that night simmered and sang, and sang this one sweet song for Sandy.

He took the first opportunity after supper to slip out and away from Limber Tim; and there in the dark, with his face to the great black forest, he stood saying over and over to himself, in his great coarse voice, trying to catch the soft tones of the Widow, "You are such good company."

That evening Limber Tim leaned up against the logs of the Howling Wilderness, and told all that had happened, and how Sandy had seen the Widow, how he had sat in her cabin, how he had talked, and how she had smiled, and what a very hero his "pardner" had become. He told of Washee-Washee.

The story of Washee-Washee went through the Forks, and then the next morning the Forks rose up and "went through" Washee-Washee.

Perhaps it was what the Widow had said about the "poor little, helpless, harmless man," that saved him, but certain it was, for some unknown reason, the miners dealt gently with this strange little stranger. Had this been one or even a dozen, of their own kind, some tree in the neighborhood of the Forks would have borne in less than an hour one, or even a dozen, of strange and ugly fruit. They went to Washee-Washee's cabin. He smiled as he saw them approach, half shut his eyes as they entered, laid his head a little to one side as they tore up his bunk, and looked perfectly happy, and peaceful as a lamb, as they pulled out from under it enough old clothes to open a shop in Petticoat Lane, or even in Bow Street.

They found a rifle-blanket in one of his wooden shoes, and it was heavy with gold-dust. Poor Washee-Washee, when called upon to explain, said timidly that he had found it floating up the river past his cabin, and took it in to dry it. He seemed hurt when they refused to believe him. They found a hose coiled up in his great bamboo hat. One of the men took hold of his queue, his beautiful long black queue that swept the ground with its braided folds and black silk tassels tipped with red and gold, and found it heavy with nuggets, hidden away, for what purpose goodness only knows. It was heavy enough to sink it like a shot were it a fish line—and all this gold was his!

They threatened hard things to Washee-Washee, these rough, outraged, hairy fellows, who had patronized him and helped him and tried to get him along in the world, but he was perfectly passive and tranquil.

A man who stood there with a bundle of recovered treasure-trove, in the shape of shirts and coats of many colors, because of many patches, took Washee-Washee by the little pink ear, and twisted him up and around till he saw his face. Then he let him go, and catching his clothes up under his arm strode on out of the cabin and on down to his claim and his work. The meekest man that the world has seen since Socrates, was Washee-Washee. He sat there with the same semi-grin on his face, the same half smile in his almond eyes, though a man shook a rope in his face, jerked it up, thrust out his tongue, pointed to a tree, and hung himself in pantomime before this placid Chinaman.

"What will we do with him?" A bearded citizen stood there with a bundle of clothes under his arm, waiting to be gone.

"Poor, lonesome, harmless little man." Sandy stood there, repeating the words of the little Widow without knowing it.

"He does lie so helplessly," said one. "If he could only lie decently, we might hang him decently."

"Tell you what, flog him and send him adrift." The man who proposed this was a stranger, with an anchor and other hall-marks of the sea on his hairy arms.

"Wolves would eat 'im on the mountain."

"Wolves eat a Chinaman! They'd eat a gum boot fust!"

"Tell you what we'll do," growled the Gopher, "reform him."

"Reform hell!" said the sailor to himself.

"Come, let's do a little missionary business, and begin at home," urged the Gopher. "Get the Judge to reprimand him. Have him talk to him an hour, then let the Parson speak to him another hour. If he lives that through he will be an honest man, or if not honest he will at least be harmless."

Now they had no preacher in the Forks, not

even the semblance of one yet, neither had they a lawyer or doctor, but this Parson was a power in the camp. He was perhaps the most popular man there. He was certainly the most influential, for he was a man who could talk. They called him the Parson because he was certainly the profanest man in all the mines.

The idea was novel and was at once adopted. Here at last was a practical application of the popular feeling, in older republics, that the officers are the servants of the public.

The little Judge here was certainly the people's servant. If he had not been, if he had asserted himself at all and taken up arms and fortified himself behind a barricade of books, they would simply have called a miners' meeting in half an hour, and in half an hour would have had the little man ousted and another man in his place, and then back to their work as if nothing ever had happened. Never in the world had men known such absolute liberty as was attained here. There was not even the dominion of woman. And yet they were not happy.

They marched Washee-Washee to the Howling Wilderness, told the sentence, and called upon the Parson to enforce judgment.

He now took a cordial and began. Washee-Washee sat before him on a bench, leaning against the wall. The little man seemed as if he was about to go to sleep; possibly his conscience had kept him awake the night before, when he found that all his little investments had been a failure in the Forks.

The Parson began. Washee-Washee flinched, jerked back, sat bolt upright, and seemed to suffer.

Then the Parson shot another oath. This time it came like a cannon ball, and red hot too, for Washee-Washee was almost lifted out of his seat.

Then the Parson took his breath a bit, rolled the quid of tobacco in his mouth from left to right and from right to left, and as he did so he selected the very broadest, knottiest, and ugliest oaths that he had found in all his fifty years of life at sea and on the border.

Washee-Washee had lost his expression of peace. He had evidently been terribly shaken. The Parson had rested a good spell, however, and the little, slim, brown man before him, who had crawled out over the great wall of China, sailed across the sea of seas, climbed the Sierras, and sat down in their midst to begin the old clothes business, without pay or promise, was again settling back, as if about to surrender to sleep.

Cannon balls! conical shot! chain shot! and

shot red hot! Never were such oaths heard in the world before! The Chinaman fell over.

"Stop!" cried the bar-keeper of the Howling Wilderness, who did n't want the expense of the funeral; "stop! do you mean to cuss him to death?"

The Chinaman was allowed time to recover, and then they sat him again on the bench. A man fanned him with his broad bamboo hat, lest he should faint before the last half of the punishment was nearly through, and the Judge was called upon to enforce the remainder of their sentence.

The Judge come forward slowly, put his two hands back under his coat tails, tilted forward on his toes and began:

"Washee-Washee! In this glorious climate of Californy — how could you?"

Washee-Washee nodded, and the Judge broke down badly embarrassed. At last he recovered himself, and began in a deep, earnest and entreating tone:

"Washee-Washee, in this glorious climate of Californy you should remember the seventh Commandment, and never, under any circumstances or temptations that beset you, should you covet your neighbor's goods, or his boots, or his shirt, or his socks, or his handkerchief, or any thing that is his, or —"

The Judge paused, the men giggled, and then they roared, and laughed, and danced about their little Judge; for Washee-Washee had folded his little brown hands in his lap, and was sleeping as sweetly as a baby in its cradle.

CHAPTER VI.

SOME UNWRITTEN HISTORY.

THE murder of Joseph Smith, the so-called prophet, meant more than any other similar event in history. This man, as well as his brother, Hiram, was not only an honest, brave gentleman, but also a man of culture and refinement. The latter, it may not be generally known, was a candidate for Congress, when that place was counted the post of honor.

Nothing in the New World ever so intensified the minds of men as the life and death of this singular man, Joseph Smith. On the one hand he was hated to death, on the other hand he was adored while living, worshiped when dead. Men for his memory's sake burned their bridges behind them, as it were, and fled destitute to the wilderness.

With no capital but a hoe and a wheelbarrow, they built up, in a quarter of a century, in the middle of a desert, the most remote and the most remarkable commonwealth that the world has ever seen. Salt Lake City was the one pier upon which was laid the long and unbroken iron chain of the Pacific Railroad.

On what singular foundations lie the corner stones of some of the greatest achievements! I think you can safely say that had there been no Joseph Smith there had been, up to this date at least, no Pacific Railroad.

This tragedy meant everything to those who took part in it, no matter on which side they fought or followed.

No one saw beyond the circle of houses in which they then lived and moved. As a rule those who followed the prophet, as well as those who murdered him, were wild, ignorant men, from the mountains of Tennessee, the wilds of Virginia and their own Missouri.

To these men, as I have said, this tragedy meant all the world. Carthage to them meant all that Carthage ever meant to Rome.

Nearly a hundred men, heavily masked, moving down upon a prison, with its half dozen inmates. A little tussle; one struggle at the door. Then a few shots. Then a few men lying in their blood on the prison floor. Then a leap from a window, a fall; a man lying dead in the jail yard. Some masked men pick up the body. They sit it up against a pump in the yard; and then they, as if to be doubly certain, fire at the dead body of the prophet as they file out of the jail yard and disappear.

All is consternation, terror now, flight! It seems there will not be one human being, save the dead and dying, left in the town. One family alone dares to remain to care for the murdered.

The work was well done. If such a deed can be done well, this certainly was. The secret was kept as never had secret been kept before. Life was depending. Not only the life of the man who had taken part, but the lives of his children, his wife, all his house. Who says the West is not the world of Romance and Tragedy?

A pendulum must swing about as far one way as it does the other. Blood meant blood. From the stains on that prison floor sprang the Dragon's teeth. Out of that awful day came forth a singular conception: the Danites—Destroying Angels.

The prophet of God, as these men professed, had been slain. Unlike the Christians, they proposed to slay in revenge.

I fancy you might trace this on till you came to the awful tragedy of Mountain Meadows. Putting the two tragedies together, side by side, and passing them on to the impartial judgment of some pagan, I am not certain that he would not pronounce in favor of the Mormon.

History trenches closely upon romance, and here we must leave the very uncertain and crudely traced outline of the former and follow on in the latter, as we began.

The story runs that the Danites found trace of one man who had taken an active part in the death of their prophet. His name was Williams, and was a man of a large and refined family.

Williams in the course of a year was found dead — drowned! Drowned he certainly was, but whether by accident or the design of enemies (for suicide does not sever the life of the borderer) was not known. Then his eldest son was found dead in the woods. His empty rifle was in his hand. He too might have perished either by accident or design. The mother was the next victim. There was consternation in the family; in all the settlement.

Another victim! Then another! Now it was certain that some awful agency was at work, and that the family was doomed. The only hope of safety lay in flight. One night the four surviving children, three grown sons and a daughter, set out to cross the plains. They had a team of strong horses, and pushed on in the hope of falling in with some train of emigrants, joining them, and thus blending in with and mixing with their members, throw the enemy from off the track.

They found their train, joined it, crossed the Missouri River, and moving on, began to deem themselves secure.

Soon it came the turn for one of the brothers to stand guard. He kissed his pale, sad sister, as he shouldered his gun and went on duty. And it was well that he said good-bye, for he was never heard of afterwards.

As they neared the Rocky Mountains, a party of half a dozen rode out from the train to take buffalo. One of the two remaining brothers was of this party. He never returned.

Now only two remained. The brother and sister often sat silent and bowed by the camp-fire, and looked sadly into each others' faces. What could they be thinking of? What was the one question in their minds? The man could only have been saying to himself, "Sister, whose turn next? is it you or I?" His brow darkened as he thought how terrible it would be to leave his sister all alone. And there was an old Roman nobility in the wish that she might die before him.

The question was not long unsettled. As they neared the Sierras, a stray shot from the willows that grow on the banks of the Humboldt, laid the brother dead at his sister's feet.

Nancy Williams was now left alone. One day, as they ascended the Sierras, she too was missed. Little was said. People feared to speak. There was something terrible in this persecution to the death in the dark. Who were these men, and where? Did they sit at your very elbow in camp, and dip from the same dish? They too could keep secrets as well as the assassins of their so-called prophet.

What had become of Nancy Williams? Had she too really been murdered? or had she in terror stolen away in disguise, and made her way into the mines alone? No one knew. People soon became too much concerned with their own affairs, as they neared the gold-fields, and men only now and then thought of the name of Nancy Williams.

One day two strange men entered the Howling Wilderness saloon, and spoke in signs and monosyllables to the cinnamon-haired bar-keeper, and pointed up toward the cabin of the "Widow." Sandy entered as these two men went out.

The bar-keeper looked at Sandy a long time, as if some great question was battling in his mind. At last, in a husky and hurried voice, he said, as he looked out through the door, and over his shoulder, as if he feared the very logs of the house might betray him:

"Them 's Danites."

"What in hell do they want at the Forks?" The sledge-hammer fist fell on the counter like a thunder-bolt.

"Shoo!" The red, bristled head of the bar-keeper reached over toward Sandy. The bar-keeper's hand reached out and took Sandy by the loose blue-shirt bosom, and drew him close up to the red head. Then again looking toward the door, and then back over his shoulder, as if he suspected that his own bottles might hear him, he said, in a sharp hissing whisper, "Shoo! They want Nancy Williams!"

Sandy's mind at once turned to the Widow. He dared not trust the bar-keeper. In truth, no man dared trust his best friend where this most terrible and secret order was concerned. He did not answer this man, but silently, and as unconcerned as possible, turned away and went back to his cabin.

CHAPTER VII.

THAT BOY.

AS before remarked, the boy poet, Little Billie Piper, sly and timid as he was with the men, was about the first to make friends with this first woman in this wild Eden. Men noted this as they did all things that in any way touched the life or affairs of the Widow, and made their observations accordingly.

"Thim 's a bad lot," said the Irishman, as he rested his elbow on the counter, and held his glass poised in the air; "thim 's a bad lot fur the woman, as writes poetry."

Then the son of Erin winked at the row of men by his side — winked right and left — lifted his glass, shut both his eyes, and swallowed his "tarantula juice," as they called it in the mines.

Then this man wiped his broad mouth on his red sleeve, hitched up the broad belt that supported his duck breeches, and said, with another wink:

"Jist think of Bryan; that fellow, Lord

O'Bryan. Why, gints, I tell yez he was pizen on the six."

But the Parson, the great rival of Sandy for the Widow's affections, took a deeper interest in this than that of an idle gossip.

It was with a lofty sort of derision in his tone and manner, that he now always spoke of the strange little poet, as "That Boy."

The Parson regarded him with bitter envy, as he oftentimes, at dusk and alone, saw him enter the Widow's cabin. At such times the Parson would usually stride up and down the trail, and swear to himself till he fairly tore the bark from the trees.

On one occasion, the boy returning to his own cabin at an earlier hour than usual, was met in the trail, where it ran around the spur of the mountain, on a high bluff, by the infuriated Parson.

Little Billie, as was his custom, gave him the trail, all of the trail, and stood quite aside on the lower hillside, to let him pass.

But the Parson did not pass on. He came close up to the boy as he stood there alone in the dusk, half trembling with fear, as the Parson approached.

The strong man did not speak at first. His face was terrible with rage and a strange tumult of thought.

The stars were half hidden by the sailing clouds, and the moon had not risen. It was almost dark. Away up on the mountain side a wolf called to his companion, and a lonesome night-bird, with a sharp cracked voice, kept up a mournful monotone in the cañon below.

The boy began to tremble, as the man towered up above him, and looked down into his uplifted face.

"By God, youngster," muttered the man between his teeth. The boy sank on his knees, as he saw the Parson look up and down the trail, as if to make sure that no one was in sight.

Then he reached his great hand and clutched him sharp by the shoulder:

"Come here! come! come with me!"

The broad hand tightened like a vice on the shoulder. The boy tried to rise, but trembled and half fell to the ground. The infuriated, half monster man, held tight to his shoulder, and led toward the precipice.

The boy, half lifted, half led, half dragged, found himself powerless in the hands of the Parson, and was soon on the brink of the cañon.

"Now sir, damn you, what have you been doing at the Widow's?"

The boy stood trembling before him.

"Boy! do you hear; I intend to pitch you

over the rocks, and break your infernal slim little neck!"

The boy still was silent. He could not even lift his eyes. He was preparing to die.

"Now sir, tell me the truth; what have you been doing at the Widow's?"

The boy trembled like a bird in the clutches of a hawk, but could not speak.

The Parson looked up the trail and down the trail; all was silent save the roar of the water in the cañon below, the interrupted howl of the wolf on the hill, and the mournful and monotonous call of the night-bird. He looked up through the cañon at the sky. It was a dark and cloudy night. Now and then a star stood out in the fresco of clouds, but it was a gloomy night.

"Now you look here," and he shook the boy by the shoulder and laughed like a demon. "Don't you know that if you go on this way you will fall over this bluff some night and break your cussed little neck? Don't you know that? You boy! You brat!"

Still the boy could not speak or even lift his face.

"I'll save you the trouble," said the Parson between his teeth. "'The boys' will rather like it. They will say they knew you would break your neck some night."

The boy did not speak, but beneath the iron clutch of the Parson settled to his knees.

"Now sir, you have just one minute. Do you see that star? When that flying cloud covers that star, then you die! and may God help you—and me."

The man's voice was husky with rage and from the contemplation of his awful crime.

"Speak boy! speak! speak but once before I murder you!"

The boy's eyes were lifted to the star, to the flying cloud that was about to cover it, and then to the eyes of the Parson, and he, trembling, half whispering, said, "Please, Parson, may I pray?"

The iron hand relaxed; the man let go his hold, and staggering back to the trail went down the hill in silence, and into the dark, where he belonged. * * * *

The two men who had entered the saloon at the Forks so mysteriously and had so terrified the bar-keeper, had disappeared. Yet Sandy, every man, knew that these men or their agents were all the time in their midst. No one knew the face of Nancy Williams; everybody knew the story of her life. At first there was terror in the camp. Could the Widow be Nancy Williams? It was decided that that was impossible. Then all was peace.

CHAPTER VIII.

SANDY'S COURTSHIP.

SWIFTLY, and very sweetly for Sandy, the days went by in the Forks; down there deep in the earth, almost in the dark of the under-world, in the cool of the forest, in the fragrance and spice and sweetness of the fir, and madrona, and tamarack for ever, dripping with dew, and dropping their fragrant gums and spices on the carpeted, mossy mountain side, filling the deep chasm with an odor found nowhere save in the heart of the Sierras, and Sandy was happy at last.

"You will please come again. You are such good company!" Sandy had come to think he was one of the best talkers in the world; and thinking so he was really able to begin to talk. Such is the tact and power, for good or ill, of woman.

Water will find its level. In this camp, in all new camps, in all new countries, new enterprises, wars, controversies — no matter what, there are certain men who come to the surface.

These come to the front, and men stand aside, and they take their place. They stay there, for they belong there. They may not come immediately; but let any great question be taken up, let it be one of enough consequence to stir up the waters, and the waters will find their level.

No man need stilt himself up, or seek applause, or friends in high places, or loud praise. If he belongs to the front he will get there in time, and will remain there when he arrives. If he does not, there is but little need for him to push and bribe and bother at all about it. He will only stand up in the light long enough to show to the world that some one has escaped from the woodcut of a comic almanac, or the Zoological Gardens, and will then sink back, to end his life in complaining of hard treatment and lack of appreciation.

Let us rather accept the situation, good or bad, play the piece out, and look to promotion in the next great drama.

Do not despise my spicy little camp in the Sierras. It was a world of itself. Perhaps it was as large as all Paradise was at the first; and then it was so new, so fresh, so fragrant, sweet, and primitive.

It was something to be the first man in that camp. Cæsar, if they have written their chronicles true, would have preferred it to the second place in Rome.

Here only the strong, clear heads towered up. It was not accident that made Sandy, or the Parson either, a head man in the Forks.

The Forks knew just how sterling, and how solid, and how sincere he was. No flattery here. There was not a penny to win by it. No applause to care for here. No public opinion to appease or woo. If a man did not like the company at the Howling Wilderness he need not put in an appearance. He could stay at home, lord of his castle, toil three hundred and sixty-five days in the year, and no man would question him or doubt his motives.

Nor was it any accident that made Limber Tim the partner of Sandy. These things have a deeper root than men suppose. Sandy was the strongest man in the camp, Limber Tim was the weakest. Nothing in nature was more natural than their present relation.

It is as remarkable as it is true, that wild beasts, even when the sexes, more decent than men, are divided from each other, mate thus. The strong bear or the strong buck companions with the weak.

This Sandy never blustered or asserted himself at all. He was born above most men of his class, and he stood at their head boldly without knowing it. Had he been born an Indian he would have been a chief, would have led in battle, and dictated in council, without question or without opposition from any one. Had he been born in the old time of kings he would have put out his hand, taken a crown, and worn it as a man wears the most fitting garment, by instinct.

Sandy was born King of the Forks. He was king already, without knowing it or caring to rule it.

There are people just like that in the world, you know,—great, silent, fearless fellows, or at least there are in the Sierra-world, and they are as good as they are great. They are there, throned there, filling up more of the world than any ten thousand of those feeble things that God sent into the world, in mercy to the poor good men who sit all day silent, and cross-legged, and in nine parts, sewing, on a table.

They will not go higher, they can not go lower. They accept the authority as if they had inherited through a thousand sires.

CHAPTER IX.

"THAT BOY" IS ILL.

HOW that courtship got on, or where and when Sandy first opened his lips, nobody ever knew. At first he took Limber Tim with him. But really Limber was so awkward in the presence of ladies, or at least so thought Sandy to himself, that he was ashamed of him.

It was a great relief to Sandy, if he had only known enough to admit it to himself, to find some one in the room more awkward than himself. Nothing is a better boon, when embarrassed, than to see some one there a bigger dolt than yourself.

Limber Tim would come in, but he would not sit down. He would go over against the wall and stand there on one leg, with his hands stuck in behind him and his head lolled to one side while his mouth fell open, with his back glued up against the wall, as if he was a sort of statuary that had made up its mind never to fall down on its face.

He would stand in that attitude till the Widow would speak to him or even smile on him, and then he would flop right over with his face to the wall, whip out a great pencil from his canvas pocket, and then slowly begin to scrawl the date, or as near as he could guess it, and sketch grotesque pictures all over the new hewn logs of the cabin.

The Widow used to call that place the Almanac, for Limber Tim knew the date and day of the year, if any man in the Forks knew it. Though it sometimes happened that when the pack-train with the provisions would come in from the outer world they would find they were two, three and even four days behind or ahead in their calculations.

At last Sandy began to get tired of Limber Tim on the wall at the Widow's. Perhaps he was in the way. At all events he "shook" him, as they called it at the Howling Wilderness, and "played it alone."

One evening Sandy had a sorry tale to tell the little woman. She listened as never she had listened before. Poor Little Billie, young Piper the boy poet, the boy who was always so alone, was down with a fever, and was wild and talking in strange ways, and they had no help, no doctor, nothing. "Yes, yes," cried Sandy, "the Forks is a doin' its level best.

Watchin' and a watchin', but he won't git up ag'in. It's all up with poor Billie."

And all the Forks was doing its best too. But the boy was very ill. The Forks was good: and it was also very sorry, for it had laughed at this young man with hands white and small and a waist like a woman's, and now that he was dying it wanted to be forgiven.

It was something to the Forks that it had allowed this boy to bear his own Christian name; the only example of the kind on its records.

The Widow was not very talkative after that, and Sandy went away earlier than usual. He thought to drop in and see the boy; but turned aside and called at the Howling Wilderness. In a few minutes he went back to the cabin of the sufferer. Gently he lifted the latch, and on tip-toe he softly entered the room where he lay.

The man was utterly amazed. The Widow sat there, holding his hands now, now pushing back the soft long hair from his face, folding back the blankets, cooling his hot brow with her soft fresh hand, and looking into his eyes all the time with a tenderness that was new to Sandy.

The boy was wild with the fever, and weak and helpless. Men stood back around the wall and in the dark; they had not dared to speak to her as she entered. They were so amazed that a woman would dare do this thing—to come in among them alone, take this boy in her arms, wave them back—wild beasts as they were, they stood there mute with amazement and devotion.

"I will go now!" The boy then reached his hands and tried to rise up. "I will go away up, up, out of it all. I do n't fit in here. I do n't belong here. I don't know the people, and the people do n't know me."

Then he was still, and his mind wandered in another direction, when he began again.

"Now I will go; and I will go alone. I am so, so tired. I am so hot and thirsty here. I will cross on the cool mountain and rest as I go."

The woman looked in his face, took his face in her hands as she sat by the bed, raised him tenderly and talked in a low soft voice all night long; soft and sweet and tender to the stranger as the voice of a mother.

She held his hand all night, as if she would hold him back from crossing over the river, and talked to him tenderly as if to draw him back to earth.

The gray dawn came at last, stealing down the mouth of the great black chimney, through the little window in the wall, where a paper did the duty of a pane, and there the men still stood in a row around the walls of the cabin, and there the Widow still sat holding the boy's hand, cooling his brow, calling him back to the world.

And he came. He opened his eyes and knew his fellow-men, for these fevers of the mountain are sudden and severe, and their work is soon done or abandoned.

After that the camp had a patron saint. The Parson fell ill next, but the boys rated him so soundly about his motive — as if any man could have a motive in falling ill — that he fell to cursing, and cursed himself into a perspiration, and so got well.

One morning the Widow found a nugget of gold on her doorstep. What particular goose of the camp had laid that great gold egg before her door she did not know. Maybe, after all, it was only the devotion of some honest, clear-headed man, some wealthy, fortunate fellow who wanted to quietly reward her for her noble deeds in the day of trouble.

Then came another nugget, and then another. She laid them in a row on her mantel-piece, and men (for visitors were not so infrequent now as at first) would come in, handle them, make their observations, guess from what claim this one came or that; and no man there ever told or hinted or in any way remarked that he had sent this or that, or had had any part in the splendid gifts that lay so carelessly on the little Widow's mantel-piece.

The little dreamer, the boy-poet, was once more seen on the trail with his pick and pan looking for gold in the earth by day, for gold in the skies at night. But never a word did he whisper of the awful threat of the Parson.

CHAPTER X.

A SCENE IN THE SIERRAS.

TO the amazement of all the Forks, one day, when a bearded man in gum boots, slouch hat, and blue shirt, reached in at the Widow's for his washing, the hand that reached it out was not the Widow's. It was the little brown lazy hand of Washee-Washee.

Of course the camp did not like this. This Chinaman to them was a sort of eclipse, a dark body passing between the miners and their sun. They remonstrated, and the Parson bore the remonstrance to the Widow in a speech of his own; and, to his own great surprise it was not ornamented with a single oath.

" The Forks began his reformation; let me go on with it. Why not?" answered the woman.

" You will be plundered."

" Of what?"

The Parson looked at the gold nuggets on the mantel-piece, and shifted the quid of tobacco from right to left.

"Washee-Washee will lie," began the Widow soberly. "He can lie, and he does lie, very cheerfully and very rapidly, in spite of his name, which might suggest better things; but he steals no more — do you, little brownie?"

Washee-Washee's little black eyes glistened with gratitude. The little pagan was coming up in the social scale. The Widow had begun her missionary business where all the world ought to begin it — at home.

The Parson went away. He felt that somehow his footing with the Widow was shaken, and that he must do something to redeem the day.

The Parson was always trying to do something original. He concluded to "lay for" the Chinaman.

He took a fresh quid of tobacco, stowed himself away in the bush, and waited.

In the twilight, the mournful, the sad, but beautiful ghost of the great golden days of the Sierras, a hand reached out and took Washee-Washee by the queue as a man would take a tethered horse by the lariat.

The little man did not smile as before. He even struck back with his little brown bony hands. He wound one of them in the Parson's beard, and shouted aloud to the empty woods. The valor of honesty was on him.

However, kick as he might and shout as he could, it all did but little good, and the Parson proceeded very coolly to take him by the two heels, hold him up in the trail, and shake him in a smooth level part of it, just as if he was about to empty a bag, and did not wish to waste the contents.

Now the Parson was not at all vicious on this occasion; he had no wish to harm the Chinaman: he only wished to help the Widow. He shook Washee-Washee in perfect confidence that he would find all the gold nuggets, half the spoons, and nearly all the household goods in the little Widow's warm and sparely furnished room. He had not been a bit surprised if he had shaken out the Widow's goods and wares, her wash-tub, and clothes-line. "Ah, certainly," said the Parson, pausing, to himself, "for is not Washee-Washee's line the clothes-line?"

Shake, shake, shake. It was of no use. Something had fallen from his blue blouse, but it was not gold. He stood the little man down, with the other end up, and was a bit angry that he did not go on smiling as before.

He stooped, and picked up the little black object that had been shaken from the brown little fellow before him. The Parson began to swear. It was only a little ten-cent Testament, in diamond type, with a cloth cover. The

Parson put his head to one side, filliped the leaves with his thumb and finger, and then, feeling perfectly certain that it did not belong to any of the boys in the camp, and equally certain that it was not an article that he cared to carry around loose with him, he filliped the leaves again, and, handing it back to Washee-Washee, said, "Git!"

The Parson took one end of the trail, and the little pagan the other.

A Missourian who lay in his bunk up against the wall, smoking his pipe of "pigtail" after supper, looked out from his cabin window through the wood and up towards the Parson's cabin, where the trail wound on the hillside above him.

"It's a thunderin' and a lightnin' like cats and dogs. There's a-gwyne to be a storm to-night."

But it was only the Parson swearing at his bad luck and that Chinaman.

"Only a Testament!" Then an idea struck him like an inspiration. Did not the good little Widow give the brown wretch this thing?

He stopped swearing, stood still in the trail a moment, and then, giving a long whistle as he drew a long breath, he went on to his cabin in silence.

That Testament troubled the Parson. There

was not much religion in the Forks. There was little sign of anything of that kind among the men of the Sierras. Perhaps there were other Testaments hidden away under the bunks of the miners, but they were never visible. I know of one, the gift of a good mother, that forever refused to get lost, or wear out, or disappear under any circumstances. Other books would get themselves borrowed and never come back, other books would get themselves thrummed and thumbed, the backs torn off, and the leaves torn out, but this one little book with its black, modest cover was always the same. It looked as new and nice, as ready to be read, as full of hope and promise, after ten years of service in the Sierras, as it did the day it first nestled down in the bottom of the carpet-bag to wait patiently for the prodigal to return and feed upon its glorious promises.

But the presence of this book had a wider meaning than all this to the Parson.

Williams had been a sort of Calvin. He was a terrible religious enthusiast. It was his devotion, his misled enthusiasm, that made him take part in the persecution and death of the so-called prophet. It was that which brought the awful persecution upon him and his. The children, it was said, inherited their father's religious zeal.

This Testament was to the Parson only another evidence that the Widow was indeed the missing Nancy Williams. He told all this in confidence to a knot of friends the next day.

Deboon only brushed and brushed, with both hands, a pet fox which perched friskily on his shoulder, but said nothing.

The Gopher slowly arose and shook himself. Then he reached out his fist and shook it in the air.

"What if she is? By the eternal Tom Cats! What if she is the real living and breathing Nancy Williams? And what if they do say she killed one of 'em the night before she got away, eh? Here she is and here she stays, and let me see the Destroying Angel, Danite or Devil, that dares to interfere."

The man strode out of the cabin like a king, and Deboon only stroked his frisky fox and walked on after him, looking back quietly at the little crowd over his shoulder.

Yet for all that, these men who were so brave and defiant in open fight, were awed and almost terrified by the strange and mysterious order that moved so secretly and so certainly upon its victims, and no other man there gave any expression to his thoughts.

CHAPTER XI.

THE PARSON'S PURSUIT OF LOVE.

BUT the Danites did not again openly appear. The Widow it seemed was now secure, and the men began to forget that they had ever counted her the last of the doomed family, or suspected that there was blood on her hands.

As the Summer wore away, her suitors dropped off like early candidates for office, and left the field almost entirely to the two leading men of the camp — Sandy and the Parson.

Sandy was a man of magnificent stature, with a graceful flow of sandy beard, but, as I have said, an awkward child of nature. A born leader of men, but a man who declined to lead unless forced to come to the front by his fellows and for the time take charge of whatever matter was under consideration in the camp. Sandy was a man you believed in, trusted, and honored from the first. There was not a crafty fiber or thought in his physical or mental make-up.

The Parson was a successful miner; a massive,

Gothic man, though not so tall as Sandy. He had been a sailor, I think. At all events, he had a blue band of Indian ink, with little diamonds of red set in between the bands, on his left wrist. Possibly it was his right wrist, for I can not recall positively at this distance of time, but I think it was the left.

The Parson was the first authority in history, politics, theology, anything whatever that came up. I do not think he was learned; but he was always so positive, and always so ready with his opinions, and always so ready to back them up too, that all were willing to ask his opinion in matters of doubt, and few were willing to question his replies.

After awhile it became talked about that Sandy was losing ground with the Widow — or, rather, that the Parson was having it pretty much his own way there, as in other things in the camp, and that Sandy rarely put in an appearance.

A year went by and then a pretty little cottage began to peep through the trees from a little hill back of town; and then it came out that this, with its glass windows and green window-blinds, was the property of the Parson, and destined as the home of the Widow.

I think the camp was rather pleased at this. True there was a bit of ambition and a grain of cunning too in the Parson's nature, which made the free, wild men of the mountains look upon him sometimes with less favor than they did on Sandy. Still some of them liked him, and all were glad that the Widow was to have a home at last.

But somehow the wedding did not come on as soon as was expected, and the Widow kept on rubbing, rubbing, day after day, week after week, as if nothing of the kind was ever to happen to her.

Late in the Fall, one evening, as the men stood in a semicircle in the Howling Wilderness saloon, with their backs to the blazing log fire, Sandy brought his fist down emphatically on the bar, as he took part in the conversation, and, turning to the crowd, said:

"It's an everlastin' and a burnin' shame!"

He rested his right elbow on the bar, and drew the back of his left hand across his mouth, as if embarrassed, and again began:

"It's a breathin' and a burnin' shame, I say, that the woman has got for to go on in this way, a washin' of duds for us fellows of this here camp. If this here camp can't afford one lady in its precincts, why, then I shall pull up stakes and go to where the tall cedars cast their shadows over the coyote, and the coyote howls and howls—and—and—"

He wiped his mouth again, and broke down utterly. But he had said enough. A responsive chord was touched, and the men fairly sprang to their feet with delight at the thought.

Some of the best things in life are like leads of gold — we come upon them in a kind of sudden discovery.

The Parson's eyes twinkled with delight. "I move that Sandy take the chair for this occasion, and second the motion, and plank down twenty ounces for the Widow."

Sandy removed his slouch hat, blushed behind his beard at the new dignity, and said:

"Bully for you! I raise you five ounces and ante the dust."

Here he drew a long, heavy purse from his pocket, and passed it over to the bar-keeper, who thereby became treasurer of the enterprise without further remark. The Parson's eye twinkled again.

"I see your five ounces and go you ten better."

"Called," said Sandy, and he pecked at the bar-keeper, which little motion of the head meant that that further amount was to be weighed from the purse for the benefit of the Widow.

One by one the boys came forward; and, as the enterprise got noised about the camp, they came down to the Howling Wilderness saloon till far in the night, to contribute what they called their "Widow's mite."

Even the head man of the company up the creek known as the "Gay Roosters," and who was notoriously the most rough and reckless man in the camp, jumped a first-class poker game, where he was playing at twenty dollars ante and pass the buck, to come in and weigh out dust enough to "call" the Parson and Sandy.

The Forks felt proud of itself for the deed. Men slept sounder and awoke in a better humor with themselves for the act.

Yet all this time it was pretty well conceded that the gold, and the Widow too, would very soon fall to the possession of the Parson.

"Set 'em deep, Parson! Set 'em deep!" said the head of the Gay Roosters, as he shook hands with the Parson that night, winked at the "boys," and returned to his game of poker.

There had been many a funeral at the Forks; but never a birth or a wedding. But now this last, with all its rites and mysteries, was about to come upon the Forks; and the Forks felt dignified and elated. Not one of all these thousand bearded men showed unconcern. It was the great topic — the Presidential campaign, the Dolly Varden of the day. The approaching wedding was the morning talk, the talk at noon, and the talk at night.

And it was good for the camp. The last fight was forgotten. Monte took a back seat in the minds of these strange, strong men ; and, if the truth could be told, I dare say the German undertaker, who had set up under the hill, noted a marked decline in his business.

The "boys" were with the Parson, and the Parson with the "boys." They all conceded that he was a royal good fellow, and that the Widow could not well do better.

The amount of gold raised by the men in their sudden and impulsive charity was in itself, for one in the Widow's station, a reasonable fortune.

"What if she gits up and gits ?"

The man who said that was a narrow-minded, one-eyed, suspicious fellow, who barely escaped being knocked down by the head of the "Gay Roosters," and kicked into the street by the crowd.

There was a poor Dutchman in the camp who had been crippled in the first settlement of the camp, and who had been all the time too lame to work and too poor to go away.

The Parson and Sandy were sent in a committee to the Widow with the gold. She smiled, took the heavy bag in her hand, turned, shut the door in their faces, but did not say a word. That evening she was seen to enter the crippled Dutchman's cabin. The next day the crippled Dutchman rode up the trail out of camp, and was seen no more.

Still later in the Fall the Parson sat in the Howling Wilderness, with his back to the blazing, crackling fire, having it all his own way at his favorite game of old sledge.

He had led his queen for the jack just as though he knew where every card in the pack was entrenched. Then he led the king with like composure, and was just crooking his fingers up his sleeve for the ace, when a man in black, with a beaver hat and white necktie, rode by the window on a black horse.

"Somebody's a dyin' up the creek, I 'speck," said Stubbs. "Maybe it's old Yallar. He allers was a kind of a prayin' codfish eatin' cuss, any how."

Here Stubbs turned and kicked nervously at the fire.

The game did not go on after that. No one said any thing. Perhaps that was the trouble. The men fell to thinking, and the game lost its interest.

There was no fight of importance at the Howling Wilderness that night, and by midnight the frequenters of the saloon had withdrawn. The candles were then put out, and the proprietors barricaded the door against belated drunkards, spread their blankets on a monte-table, with their pistols under their heads, and by the smouldering fire were at rest.

The ground was frozen hard next morning, and the miners flocked into the Howling Wilderness. The Parson was leading off gaily again, and swearing with unusual eloquence and brilliancy, when a tall, thin, and sallow man, from Missouri, known as the "Jumper," entered. He looked wild and excited, and stepped high, as if on stilts.

The tall, thin man went straight up to the bar, struck his knuckles on the counter, and nodded at the red bottle before him. It came forward, with a glass tumbler, and he drank deep, alone and in silence.

When a miner of the Sierras enters a saloon where other men are seated, and drinks alone, without inviting any one, it is meant as a deliberate insult to those present, unless there is some dreadful thing on his mind.

The Jumper, tall and fidgety, turned to the Parson, bent his back against the counter, and pushed back his hat. Then he drew his right sleeve across his mouth, and let his arms fall down at his side limp and helpless, and his round, brown butternut head rolled loose and awkward from shoulder to shoulder.

"Parson."

"Well! well! Spit it out!" cried the Parson, as he arose from the bench, with a dreadful oath. "Spit it out! What in h—l is busted now?"

"Parson."

Here the head rolled and the arms swung more than ever, and the man seemed in dreadful agony of mind.

The Parson sprang across the room and caught him by the shoulder. He shook him till his teeth rattled like quartz in a mill.

"The—the man in black," gasped the Jumper. "The black man, on the black horse, with a white choker." The Parson looked blank, and staggered back, as the man, gasping for breath, concluded: "Well, he's gone back; and he won't marry yer. Cause why, he says Sandy says yer got one wife now any how, in Missouri, and maybe two."

The Parson sunk into a seat, dropped his face in his hands for a moment, trembled only a little, and arose pale and silent. He did not swear at all. I am perfectly certain he did not swear. I know we all spoke of that for a long time afterward, and considered it one of the most remarkable things in all the strange conduct of this man.

When the Parson arose the Jumper shook himself loose from the counter, and tilted across to the other side of the room, to give him place.

The stricken man put his hands on the counter, peeked over the bar-keeper's shoulder at his favorite bottle, as if mournfully to a friend, but said not a word. He emptied a glass, and then, without looking right or left, opened the door, and went straight up to the Parsonage. The Parsonage was the name the boys gave to the cottage on the hill among the trees.

"Gone for his two little bull-pups," said Stubbs. That was what the Parson called his silver-mounted derringers.

"There will be a funeral at the Forks to-morrow," gasped the Jumper.

Here the German undertaker arose cheerfully, and went down to his shop.

"Well, Sandy is no sardine. Bet your boots Sandy ai n't no sardine!" said Stubbs. "And, any how, he 's got the start just a little, if the Parson does nail him. For he 's won her heart; and that 's a heap, I think, for wimmen 's mighty scace in the mines — sumthin' to die for, you bet."

CHAPTER XII.

GRIT.

THE Parson was absent for hours, and the Howling Wilderness began to be impatient.

"He 's a heelin himself like a fighting-cock," said Stubbs; "and if Sandy do n't go to kingdom come with his boots on, then chaw me up for a shrimp."

The man here went to the door, opened it, put his head out in the frosty weather, and peered up the creek for Sandy, and across the creek for the Parson, but neither was in sight.

The "Gay Rooster" company knocked off from their work, with many others, and came to town in force to see the fight. The Howling Wilderness was crowded and doing a rushing business.

The two bar-keepers shifted and carefully arranged the sand-bags under the counter, which in that day and country were placed there in every well-regulated drinking saloon, so as to intercept whatever stray bits of lead might be thrown in the direction of their bodies, in the coming battle, and calmly awaited results.

About dark, a thin blue smoke, as from burning paper, curled up from the chimney of the Parsonage, and the Parson came slowly forth.

"Blamed if he has n't been a makin of his will and a burnin of his letters. Looks grummer than a deacon, too," added the man, as the Parson neared the saloon.

He spoke quietly to the boys, as he entered, but did not swear. That was thought again remarkable indeed.

He went up to the bar, tapped on the counter with his knuckles, threw his head back over his shoulder toward the crowd, and yet apparently without seeing any one, and said:

"Boys, fall in line, fall in line. Rally around me once again."

They fell in line, or at least the majority did. Some, however, stood off in little knots and groups on the other side, and pretended not to have heard or noticed what was going on. These it was at once understood were fast friends of Sandy's, and unbelievers in the Parson.

The glasses were filled quietly, slowly, and respectfully, almost like filling a grave, and then emptied in silence.

Again it was observed that the Parson did

not swear. That was considered as remarkable as the omission of prayer from the service in a well-regulated church, and, I am sure, contributed to throw a spirit of restraint over the whole party friendly to the Parson. Besides, it was noticed that he was pale, haggard, had hardly a word to say, and most of all, had barely touched the glass to his lips.

No one, however, ventured to advise, question, or in any way disturb him. All were quiet and respectful. It was very evident that the feeling in the Forks, at first, was largely with Sandy.

But Sandy did not appear that evening. This, of course, was greatly against him. The Forks began to suspect that he feared to take the responsibility of his act, and meet the man he had so strangely defamed, and, to all appearances, so deeply injured.

The next day the saloon was crowded more densely than before. Men stood off in little knots and groups, talking earnestly. There was but one topic — only the one great subject — the impending meeting between the two leading men of the camp, and the probable result.

The Parson was among the first present that day, pale and careworn. They treated him with all the delicacy of women. Not a word was said in his presence of his misfortune, or the occasion of their meeting. To the further credit of the Forks I am bound to say that there had as yet been no bets as to which one of the two men they should have to bury the next day.

The day passed, and still Sandy did not appear. Had there been any other way out of camp than through the Forks and up the rugged, winding, corkscrew stairway of rocks opposite, and in the face of the town, it might have been suspected that he had taken the Widow and fled to other lands.

The Parson came down a little late next morning, pale and quiet, as before. He did not swear. This time, in fact, he did not even drink. He sat down on a bench behind the monte-table, with his back to the fire and his face to the door. The men respectfully left a rather broad lane between the Parson and the door, and the monte-table was not patronized.

The day passed;—dusk, and still Sandy did not appear. By this time he had hardly three friends in the house.

"Has n't got the soul of a chicken!" "Caved in at last!" "Gone down in his boots!" "Busted in the snapper!" "Lost his grip!" "Do n't dare show his hand!" These and like expressions, thrown out now and then from the little knots of men here and there, were the certain indications that Sandy had lost his place in the hearts of the leading men of the Forks.

Toward midnight the bolt lifted!

Shoo!

The door opened, and Sandy entered, backed up against the wall by the door, and stood there, tall and silent.

His great beard was trimmed a little, his bushy hair carefully combed behind his ears, and the neck-tie was now subdued into a neat love-knot, in spite of its old persistent habit of twisting around and fluttering out over his left shoulder. His eye met the Parson's but did not quail.

The bar-keeper settled down gracefully behind the bags of sand, so that his eyes only remained visible above the horizon.

The head of the "Gay Roosters" tilted a table up till it made a respectable barricade for his breast, and the crowd silently settled back in the corners, packed tighter than sardines in a tin box.

You might have heard a mouse, had it crossed the floor. Even the fretful fire seemed to hold for the time its snappish red tongue, and the wind without to lean against the door and listen.

The Parson slowly arose from the table. He

had his right hand in his pocket, and was very pale.

Experienced shootists, old hands at mortal combat with their kind, glanced from man to man, measured every motion, every look, with all the intense eagerness of artists who are favored with one great and especial sight, not to be met again. Others held their heads down, and only waited in a confused sort of manner for the barking of the bull-dogs.

Neither of Sandy's hands were visible; but, as the Parson took a few steps forward, and partly drew his hand from his pocket, Sandy's right one came up like a steel spring, and the ugly black muzzle of a six-shooter was in the Parson's face.

Still he advanced, till his face almost touched the muzzle of the pistol. He seemed not to see it, or to have the least conception of his danger.

It was strange that Sandy did not pull. Maybe he was surprised at the singular action of the Parson. Perhaps he had his eye on the unlifted right hand of his antagonist. At all events he had the "drop," and could afford to wait the smallest part of a second, and see what he would do.

"I have been a-wait-ing"—the Parson halted and paused at the participle. "I have been a-wait-ing for you, Sandy, a long time."

His voice trembled. The voice that had thundered above a hundred bar-room fights, and had directed the men through many a difficulty in camp, was now low and uncertain.

"Sandy," he began again, and he took hold of the counter with his left hand, "I am-a-going-a-way. Your cabin will be too small now, and I want you to promise me to take care of the Parsonage till I come back."

Sandy sank back closer still to the wall, and his arm hung down at his side.

"You will move into the Parsonage when it is all over. It's full of good things for Winter. You will take it, I say, at once. Promise me that."

The Parson's voice was a little severe here—more determined than before; and, as he concluded, he drew the key from his pocket and handed it to Sandy.

"You will?"

"Yes."

The men looked a moment in each other's eyes. Perhaps they were both embarrassed. The door was convenient. That seemed to Sandy the best way out of his confusion, and he opened it softly and disappeared. The Howling Wilderness was paralyzed with wonder.

The Parson looked a little while out in the dark, through the open door and was gone. There was a murmur of disappointment behind him.

"Do n't you fear!" at last chimed in the head of the "Gay Roosters." "Do n't you never fear! That old sea-dog, the Parson, is deeper than a infernal gulf."

"Look here!" He put up his finger to the side of his nose, after a pause, and stroking his beard mysteriously, said: "I say, look here! Shoo! Not a word! Softly now! Powder! That 's what it means. Powder! Gits 'em both into the Parsonage and blows 'em to kingdom come together!"

The Howling Wilderness was reconciled. It was certain that the end was not yet, by a great deal. It was again struck with wonder, however; and, for want of a better expression, took a drink and settled down to a game of monte.

Early next morning — a morning full of unutterable storms and drifts of snow — Sandy entered the Widow's cabin.

The Parson was not to be seen either at the Howling Wilderness or about his own house.

Men stood about the door of the Howling Wilderness, and up and down the single street, in little knots, noting the course of things at the Parsonage, and now and then shaking their loose blanket coats and brushing off the fast falling snow.

After a while, when the smoke rose up from the chimney-top, and curled above the Parsonage with a home-like leisure, as if a woman's hand tended the fire below, a man with his face muffled up was seen making his way slowly up the rugged way that led from town across the Sierra.

It was a desperate and dangerous undertaking at that season of the year. He made but poor headway against the storm that came pelting down in his face from the fields of eternal snow; but he seemed determined, and pushed slowly on. Sometimes it was observed he would turn, and, shading his eyes from the snow, look down intently at the peaceful smoke drifting through the trees above the Parsonage.

"Some poor idiot will pass in his checks to-night, if he do n't come back pretty soon," said Stubbs, as he nodded at the man up the hill, brushed the snow from his sleeves, and went back into the saloon.

There were now two subjects of conversation in the camp; the departure of the Parson and the courtship of Sandy.

One day, however, there was quite a riffle in

the usually smooth current of affairs. It was this. A busy meddling man was seen to lay hold of Sandy, and talk a long time in a mysterious and suspicious manner. He would point to the cabin of the Widow, then to the cabin of the Poet, and gravely shake his head. The man was heard to couple the two names together. At last Sandy shook this man off, and went on his way with anything but a satisfied look.

After an open demonstration like that, the camp felt that it was privileged to speak openly what it had seriously but silently noted before. It had now three topics to talk about: the departure of the Parson, the courtship of Sandy, but now above all and chiefly the secret and frequent visits of the Poet to the Widow's cabin.

CHAPTER XIII.

AN ANNOUNCEMENT.

ONE day a miner laid his two fingers crosswise, and twisting his head to one side as he spirted a stream of tobacco juice across the saloon, said: "Sandy is a infernal fool." The men winked, and he went on. "He wants to marry that ere Widow. Wal, now, that ere Widow is in love with that ere boy. Nobody to blame. You see if the Widow loves the boy that 's the Widow's bizness, not mine; only Sandy musn't be a fool. Besides,"—and here the man's voice sank low, and he looked around as if he feared a Danite might be standing at his elbow — "besides, its my private opinion that that ere Widow is *the* Nancy Williams."

It was late in the Fall, and it certainly must have been a cold, frosty morning, for Sandy's teeth chattered together as if he had an ague, when he told the Judge.

In fact, he stood around the Howling Wilderness more than half a day, but he could not, or at least would not drink, though he did very many foolish things, and seemed ill at ease and troubled in a way that was new to him.

At last he got the Judge to one side. He took him by the collar with both hands, he backed him up in a corner, and, as he did so, his teeth chattered and ground together as if he stood half-naked on the everlasting snows that surrounded them. He pushed his face down into the red apple-like face of the magistrate, and began as if he was about to reveal the most terrible crime in the annals of the world. All the time he was holding on to the Judge with both hands, as if he feared he might not listen to his proposal, but tear away and attempt to escape.

At last Sandy drew a sharp, short breath, and blurted out what he had to say, as if it was tearing out his lungs.

"Good, good!"

The Judge drew a long breath. He swelled out to nearly twice his usual importance. You could have seen him grow.

It was now the Judge's turn to lay hold of Sandy. For now, as the great strong man had accomplished his fearful task, told his secret, and done all that was necessary to do, he wanted to get away, to go home, go anywhere and collect his thoughts, and to rest.

The Judge held him there, told him the great

advantages that would come of it, the high responsibility that he was about to put his shoulder to, and talked to him, in fact, till he grew white and stiff as a sign-post. Yet all that Sandy could remember, for almost all that he said, was something about "the glorious climate of Californy."

Never rode a king into his capital with such majesty as did the Judge the next day enter the Forks. He was swelling, bursting with the importance of his secret. But now he had Sandy's permission to tell the boys, and he went straight to the Howling Wilderness for that purpose.

His face glowed like the fire as he stood there rubbing his hands above the great mounting blaze, and bowing right and left in a patronizing sort of a way to the miners who had sauntered into the saloon.

At last the little red-faced man turned his back to the fire, stuck his two hands back behind his coat-tails, which he kept lifting up and down and fanning carelessly, as if in deep thought — stood almost tip-toe, stuck out his round little belly, and seemed about to burst with his secret.

"O this wonderful Californy climate!" He puffed a little as he said this, and fanned his coat-tails a little bit higher, perked out his belly a little bit further, and stood there as if he expected some one to speak. But as the miners seemed to think they had heard something like this before, or, at least, that the remark was not wholly new, none of them felt called upon to respond.

"Well" — the little man tilted up on his toes as he said this, and took in a long breath — "hit comes off about the next snow fall."

He had said these words one at a time, and by inches as it were, slowly, deliberately, as if he knew perfectly well that he had something to say, and that the men were bound to listen.

This time they all looked up, and half of them spoke. And oh, did n't he torture them! Not that he pretended to keep his secret of half a day — not at all! On the contrary, he kept talking on, and tip-toeing, and fanning his coat-tails, and pushing out his belly, and puffing out his cheeks, just as careless and indifferent as if all the world knew just what he was going to say, and was perfectly familiar with the subject. "Yes, gentlemen," puffed the little man, "on or about the next snow-fall the Widow, as a widow, ceases to exist. That lovely flower, my friends, is to be transplanted from its present bed to — to — into — the — O this wonderful climate of Californy!"

The Howling Wilderness was as silent as the Catacombs of Rome for nearly a minute.

Then Sandy had not been deterred either by the Widow's strange intimacy with the eccentric little Poet, or by the suspicion of the camp that this woman was the last of the doomed family.

The first thing that was heard was something like a red-hot cannon-shot. The cinnamon-headed man behind the bar dodged down behind his barricade of sandbags till only his bristling red hair and a six-shooter were visible. The decanters tilted together as if there had been an earthquake.

It was a Missourian swearing.

Somebody back in the corner said "Jer-u-salem!" — said it in joints and pieces, and then came forward and kicked the fire, and stood up by the side of the red little man, and looked down at him as if he would like to eat him for a piece of raw beef.

A fair boy, the dreamer, the poet, went back to a bunk against the further wall, where the barkeeper's bulldog lay sleeping in his blankets, and put his arms about his neck, and put his face down and remained there a long time. Perhaps he wept. Was he weeping for joy or for sorrow?

There was a great big grizzly head moved out

of the crowd and up to the bar. The head rolled on the shoulders from side to side, as if it was not very firmly fixed there, and did not particularly care at this particular time whether it remained there or not. A big fist fell like a stone on the bar. The glasses jumped as if frightened half to death; they ran up against each other, and clinked and huddled together there, and fairly screamed and split their sides in their terror. A big mouth opened behind an awful barricade of beard, again the big fist fell down, again the glasses screamed and clinked with terror, and the head rolled sidewise again, and the big mouth opened again, and the big voice said:

"By the bald-headed Elijah!" and that was all.

Then there was another calm, and you might have heard the little brown wood-mice nibbling at the old boots, and leather belts, and tin cans stowed away among the other rubbish up in the loft of the Howling Wilderness.

Then the fist came down again, and the big mouth opened, and the big mouth said, slow and loud, and long and savage, like the growl of a grizzly:

"Swaller my grandmother's boots!" Then the man fell back and melted into the crowd; and whatever romance there was in his life, whatever sentiment he may have had, whatever poetry there was pent up in the heart of this great Titan, it found no other expression than this.

The genteel gambler, who sat behind a table with its green cloth and silver faro-box, forgot to throw his card, but held his arm poised in the air till any man could have seen the Jack of Clubs, though a thousand dollars' worth of gold-dust depended on the turn.

Yet all this soon had an end, of course, and there was a confusion of tongues, and a noise that settled gradually over against the bar. Even then, it was afterwards remarked, though the men really interested did not know it at the time, that the cinnamon-headed dealer of drinks put cayenne pepper in a gin cocktail and Scheidam schnapps in a Tom and Jerry.

Limber Tim was there in their midst, but was a sad and a silent man. Perhaps he had been told all about it before, and perhaps not. Tim was not a talker, but a thinker. This to him meant the loss of his partner, the man he loved — a divorce.

Poor Limber! he only backed up against the wall, screwed his back there, twisted one leg in behind the other, stuck his hands in behind him, and so stood there till he saw a man looking at him. Then he flopped over with his face to the wall, dug up his great pencil from his great pocket, and fell to writing on the wall, and trying to hide his face from his fellows.

"Rather sudden, ai n't it, Judge?"

"Well, not so sudden — not so sudden, considerin this — this — this glorious climate of Californy."

After awhile, when the monte game had asserted itself again, and things were going on in the saloon just about as they were before the Judge made this announcement, a tall and inquisitive man with a hatchet face and a hump in his shoulder, and a twist in his neck, which made him look like an interrogation point, rose up, and reaching his neck out toward the bar, said in a sharp whisper:

"I'll bet a forty dollar hoss she's the real Nancy Williams."

The red-headed bar-keeper bristled up like a porcupine, and then put out his broad hand as if it was an extinguisher.

CHAPTER XIV.

A WEDDING IN THE SIERRAS.

THE wedding-day came. The camp had been invited to a man. There was but one place in the camp that could hold a tithe of its people, and that was the Howling Wilderness. The plan had been to have the wedding under the pines on the hill; but the wind came pitching down the mountain, with frost and snow in his beard, that morning, and drove them to the shelter.

What a place was that Howling Wilderness! It was battle-field, prize-ring, dead-house, gambling-hell, court-house, chapel, every thing by turns.

There they stood, side by side and hand in hand, before the crackling fire, before the little Judge. The house was hot. It was crowded thick as the men could stand. Tighter than sardines in a tin box, the men stood there bareheaded with hardly room to breathe. The fat little magistrate was terribly embarrassed. He had sent all the way across the mountains by the last pack-train, by the last express, by the last man who had dared the snows, but no pack-train, no express, nothing had returned with the coveted, the so-much-needed marriage ceremony and service, which he had resolved to read to the people, interspersed with such remarks and moral observations as the case might require. Alas! the form of the ceremony had not arrived. He had nothing of the kind to guide him. He had never officiated in this way before. He had never studied up in this branch.

Why should he have studied up in this line, when there was but one woman in all his little world?

As the form had not arrived, he had nothing in the world but his moral observations to use on this imposing occasion, and he was embarrassed as a man had never been embarrassed before.

He stood there trying hard to begin. He could hear the men breathe. The pretty little woman was troubled too. Her face was all the time held down, her eyes drooped, and she did not look up — did not look right or left or anywhere, but seemed to surrender herself to fate, to give herself away. Her soul seemed elsewhere, as if she sat on a high bank above all this, and was not of it or in it at all."

6

"Do you solemnly swear?"

The Judge had jerked himself together with an effort that made his joints fairly rattle. He hoisted his right hand in the air as he said this, and, having once broken ground, he went on —

"Do you solemnly swear to love, and honor, and obey?"

Poor Limber Tim, who had just room enough behind the Judge to turn over, here became embarrassed through sympathy for the little red-faced magistrate, and of course flopped over, and began to write his name and the date, and make pictures on the wall, with a nervous rapidity proportionate to his embarrassment.

"Do you solemnly swear?"

It was very painful. The little man took down his lifted flagstaff to wipe his little bald head, and he could not get it up again, but stood there still and helpless.

You could hear the men breathe deeper than before as they leaned and listened with all their might to hear. They heard the water outside gurgling on down over the great boulders, over their dams, and on through the cañon. They heard the little brown wood-mice nibble and nibble at the bits of bacon-rind and old leather boots up in the loft above their heads, but that was all. At last the Judge revived, and began again in a voice that was full of desperation:

"Do you solemnly swear to love, and protect, and honor, and obey, till death do you part; and —"

Here the voice fell down low, lower, and the Judge was again floundering in the water. Then his head went under utterly. Then he rose, and "Now I lay me down to sleep" rolled tremulously through the silent room from the lips of the Judge. Then again the head was under water, then it rose up again, and there was something like "Twinkle, twinkle, little star." Then the voice died again, again the head was under water. Then it rose again, and the head went up high in the air, and the voice was loud and resolute, and the man rose on his tiptoes, and beginning with —"When in the course of human events," he went on in a deep and splendid tone with the Declaration of Independence, to the very teeth of tyrannical King George, and then bringing his hand down emphatically on the gambling table that stood to his right, said, loud, and clear, and resolute, and authoritatively, as he tilted forward on his toes, "So help you God, and I pronounce you man and wife."

The exhausted Judge sank back against the wall on top of Limber Tim, and then, as if he all at once came to remember a part of the ceremony, and after Sandy and the Widow and all were thinking that it was quite over, he began in a low but clear voice—

"Then by virtue of the authority in me vested, and according to the laws and the statutes of the State of California in such cases made and provided, I pronounce you man and wife."

Then he rose up, came forward, and shaking the new bride by the hand, then lifting it to his lips and kissing it gallantly, he said carelessly, and as if nothing had happened, "You will pardon me for pausing occasionally as I did. The room is so warm and the ceremony is so long, that I really began to be exhausted."

He was going on to say something about the glorious climate of California, but the men came forward, crowded around in this day of all days, and quite squeezed the little man away from the "Widow," as she was still called.

It was perfectly splendid! How they did shout, and laugh, and cheer, and how careful they were to shake all the round oaths out of their speech before addressing her. And how they did crowd around, as Sandy led her away, every man of them, even to Washee-Washee, to wish her "God speed," and a long and a pleasant life in their midst, down there in the gorge, in the heart of the great Sierras.

Only two circumstances in connection with this first family of the Sierras worth mentioning, occurred for some months. The first of these was the banishment of the boy-poet from the presence of the Widow. Sandy led her at once to the "parsonage" with the green window blinds, as he had solemnly promised the Parson to do. Into this house the boy was never seen to enter. Sandy, it was whispered, had forbidden him the house. The verdict of the Camp was: Served him right.

The other little event was, to all appearances, of still less consequence. Yet it showed that there was a storm brewing, and it was a straw which showed which way the wind was blowing. The boy was seen late at night by some men who were passing, peering in at the Widow's window. He ran away like one caught in a crime. But they said he "looked pale as a ghost, and sickly, and sad, and lonesome."

CHAPTER XV.

WHAT'S THE MATTER NOW!

JUST exactly how many days or weeks or even months had blown over the Forks through the long bleak winter since the wedding no man knew. These men in the mountains, snowed up for half-a-year, where there is no business, where there is no law, no church, nothing but half-wild men hard at work — these men, I say, sometimes forget the day, the week, even the month. Yet the Day of the week is always kept. Six days they labor in the mine; the seventh, they do not rest, but they at least do not mine.

Certainly there was snow on the day of the wedding, and certain it was that there was a little fall of snow on the high hill-sides, and in the black fir tops, and the great pines were tipped in white, as Sandy hurried from his cabin down to the Forks in search of his now divorced and forgotten Limber Tim. He was pale and excited. He pushed his great black, broad hat down over his eyes as he hurried on down the trail, slipping and sliding over the worn walk, over the new sprinkle of snow, in his great big gum boots. Then he pushed his hat back so as to get the cool wind of March in his face and even the blustering snow in his beard.

He found Limber at last standing on one leg by the great log fire in the Howling Wilderness, lonesome as a crow in March. He pulled his hat again down over his eyes as he approached his old partner, and stooped his shoulders and looked out from under its rim, as if he was half afraid or else was half ashamed.

In all western towns, in all mines, in all cities, great or small for that matter, there is always one common center. Here it was the Howling Wilderness. If a man felt sad, what better place than the Howling Wilderness saloon to go to for distraction? If a man felt glad, where else could he go to share his mirth.

Here was happiness or unhappiness. All great extremes run together. Tears flow as freely for joy as for grief. Between intense delight or deepest sorrow the wall is so thin you can whisper through it and be heard.

Here, at fifty cents a glass, you had dealt out to you over a great plank laid up upon a barricade of sand-bags, that were laid there to intercept any stray bullet that might be making its way towards the crimson-headed vendor of poisons, almost any drink that you might name. And it is safe to say that all of the following popular drinks, that is Old Tiger, Bad Eye, Forty Rod, Rat Pizen, Rot Gut, Hell's Delight, and Howling Modoc, were all made from the same decoction of bad rum, worse tobacco, and first-class cayenne pepper. The difference in proportion of ingredients made the difference in the infernal drinks.

If one of those splendid, misled fellows, who really knew no better, felt very sad, he took one of these drinks; if he felt very glad he took two.

Sandy wheeled on his heel the moment he found his old friend, and went out without saying a word. He stood there in the snow, the wind twisting about his beard, blowing his old hat-rim up and down, and he seemed as one lost. At length he lifted the latch again hastily, hesitated, looked back, around, up towards his cabin on the hill, and then suddenly pushing his hat back again, as if he wanted room to breathe, he tumbled into the saloon, went right up before Limber Tim, and bringing his two hands down on his two shoulders, said tremulously, "Limber Tim."

Sandy had laid hold of him as if he had determined to never let him go again, and the man fairly winced under his great vice-like grasp. He looked at the back log on the fire, looked left and right, but did not look Sandy in the face. If he had, he would for the first time in all his timid experience have been able to have had it all his own way.

"O Limber!"

Sandy had fished up one of his hands high enough to pull his hat down over his eyes, and now nothing was to be seen but a hat rim and the fringe of a grizzly beard.

Limber Tim looked up. He never before had heard his old partner's voice troubled, and he was very sorry, and began to look, or to try to look, Sandy in the face. Up went a big hand from a shoulder, back went the old hat, and then Limber Tim looked to the left at a lot of picks and pans, and tom irons, and crevicing spoons, that lay up against the wall, but did not speak.

"Limber Tim! I tell you. My — my —"

Sandy choked. He never had yet been able to call her his wife. He had tried to do so over and over again. His dear little wife had taught him many things — had made him, in fact, another man, but she never could get him to speak of her to the other miners but as "the Widow." He had gone out by himself and practiced it in the dark to himself; he was certain he could say it in the crowd, but somehow just at the moment he tried to say it he was certain some one was thinking about it just as he was, was watching him, and so it always and for ever stuck in his throat. How he loved her! How tender he was to her all the time! How he did little else but think of her and her happiness day and night; but he had been a savage so long, had been with the "boys" so much, that he could not find it in his power to say that one dear word. It was like a new convert trying to pray in public in one of the great camp meetings of the West; or to stand up before all his neighbors and confess his sins.

He stood still only a second; in fact, all this took but a moment, for Sandy was in a terrible hurry. Limber Tim had never seen him in such a hurry before. Up shot the hand, down slid the hat, and Sandy was quite hidden away again. It was a moment of terrible embarrassment. When an Englishman is embarrassed he takes snuff; when a Yankee is embarrassed he whips out a jack-knife and falls to whittling anything that he can find, not excepting the ends of his fingers; but a true Californian of Sierras jerks his head at the boys, heads straight up to the bar, knocks his knuckles on the board, winks at the bar-keeper, pecks his nose at his favorite bottle, fills to the brim, nods his head down the line to the left, then to the right, hoists his Poison, throws back his head, and then falls back wiping his mouth with the back of his hand, quite recovered from his confusion.

Sandy backed his partner into a corner rapidly, and then, laying his hands again on his shoulders, said: "Limber Tim! she's sick!"

He had to throw his head forward to say it. It came out as if jerked from his throat by a thousand fish-hooks.

He raised his two great hands, and reaching out his face again clutched the two shoulders, and said, "She's d—d sick!"

Up went the hands, back went the hat, the door was jerked open, a man whirled out of the door as if he had been a whirlwind, up the trail, up over the stones and snow and logs. Sandy climbed to his cabin on the hill, while the boys followed him with their eyes; and then stood looking at each other in wonder as he disappeared in the door.

Through the cabin burst the man, and back to the little bedroom, as if he had been wild as the north wind that whistled and whirled about without.

The little lady lay there, quiet now, but her face was white as ashes. The blood had gone out from her face like a falling tide; the pain was over, but only, like a tide, to return.

How white she was, and how beautiful she was! How helpless she was down there in the deep, hidden in a crack of the world, away from all old friends, away from all her kindred, all her sex and kind. She was very ill, so alone was she; not a doctor this side of that great impassable belt of snow that curved away like a deep white wave around and above the heads of the three little rivers. Sandy saw all this, felt all this. It cut him to the core, and he shook like a leaf.

What a pretty nest of a bed-room! How fragrant it was from the fir-boughs that were gathered under foot. There were little curtains about this bed, there deep in the Sierras. Coarse they were, it is true, very coarse, but white as the snow that whirled about without the cabin. Still, you might have seen here and there that there were cloudy spots that had refused all the time to be quite washed out, rub and soak and soap and boil them as the Widow and Washee-Washee would.

If you had lain in that bed through a spell of sickness, and looked and looked at the curtains and all things as sick people will all the time look and look when they lie there and can do nothing else, you would at last have noticed that these coarse but snowy curtains had been made of as many pieces as Jacob's coat. And lying there and looking and looking, you would have at last in the course of time read there in one of the many cloudy spots, these words stamped in bended rows of fantastic letters:

SELF-RISING FLOUR
WARRANTED SUPERFINE.
50 LBS.

There was a little cracked piece of looking-glass on the wall, no bigger than your palm. It was fastened on the wall, over, perhaps, the only illustrated paper that had ever found its way to the Forks. There were little rosettes around this little glass that had been made from leaves of every color by the cunning hand of the Widow. There were great maple-leaves, and leaves of many trees in all the hues of Summer, hung up here and there, sewn together, and made to make the little bedroom beautiful. And what a treasure the little glass was! It seemed to be the great little center of the house. All things rallied, or seemed to be trying to rally, around it. To be sure, the Widow was not at all plain.

Plain! to Sandy she was the center of the world. The rising and the setting of the sun.

The carpet had been finished by the same cunning hand. This had been made of gunny bags sewn together with twine; and under this carpet there was a thick coat of fine fir-boughs that left the room all the time sweet and warm, and fragrant as a forest in the Spring. There were little three-legged benches waiting about in the corners; but by the bedside sat the great work of art in the camp, a rocking-chair made of elk horns. This was the gift of a rejected but generous lover.

On the little wooden mantel-piece above the fire-place there stood a row of nuggets. They lay there as if they were a sort of Winter fruit put by to ripen. They were like oranges which you see lying about the peasants' houses in Italy, and almost as large. These were the gifts of the hardy miners of the Forks to their patron saint; gifts given at such times and in such ways that they could not be well refused.

Once there had been, late in the night, a heavy stone thrown against the door, while the two "turtle doves," as the camp used to call its lovers, sat by the fire.

In less than a second Sandy's pistol stuck its nose out like a little bull-dog and began to look down the hill in the darkness.

A man leaned over the fence and laughed in his face. "Now don't do that, Sandy! now do n't." Sandy let his pistol fall half ashamed; for it was the voice of a friend.

"Good-bye, Sandy!" the man called back up the trail in the dark. "Good-bye. That 's for the Widder. Made my pile and off for Pike. Good-bye!"

When Washee-Washee went out next morning for wood, there he found lying at the door the cause of the trouble in the night. It was a great nugget of gold that the rough Missourian had thrown to his patron saint as he passed.

Once a miner sent them a great fine salmon. The Widow on opening it found it half full of gold. She took all this back to the man, whom she found seated at the green table at the Howling Wilderness, behind a silver faro box; for to mining the man also attached the profession of gambler. She laid this heap of gold down on the table before the man with the faro box and cards. The miners gathered around. The man with the silver box began to deal his cards.

"All on the single turn, Missus Sandy?"

The Judge came forward, "Do n't bet it all on the first deal, do you? That 's pretty steep, even for the oldest of us!"

"Bet! I do n't bet at all. I bring Poker Jake his money back. I found this all in the fish he sent us. It is his. It is a trick, perhaps. Fish do n't eat gold, you know."

"O yes they dus, Missus Sandy."

Poker Jake stopped with the card half turned in the air. The Widow held up her pretty finger and her pretty lips pouted as she made her little speech to the gambler, and told him she could not keep the gold. The miners gathered around in wonder and admiration.

Jake laid down his card.

"Well, can't a salmon eat gold if he likes?"

"No."

"There, Missus Sandy, y'er wrong!" argued the little Judge, and then he began to tell her the story of Jonah and the whale, and wound up with the declaration that there was nothing at all unnatural in a fish eating gold in "this glorious climate of Californy."

"Will you not take back your gold?"

"Nary a red."

There was a pale thoughtful young man, half ill, too feeble to work, to leave, to retreat from the mountains, standing by the fire when the Widow had entered the saloon. It was the boy poet.

She took up the bag of gold, turned around, looked back in the corner of the saloon, for he had retreated out of sight as she entered, saw the young man hiding back in the shade, leaning over the bunk, caressing the dog; possibly he was crying. Her face lighted with a light that was high and beautiful and half divine.

She turned, held the gold out to Poker Jake.

"No!"

"And then is it mine? all mine, to do as I like with it?"

Yours, lady. Yours to take and go home and git from out of the cañon, out of this hole in the ground, and live like a Christian, as yer are, and not live here like a wild beast in a carawan."

The man stood up as he spoke, and was proud of his speech, and the men cheered and cheered and said :

"Bully for Poker Jake ! "

Then the little Widow turned again, went back to the boy leaning over the bull-dog, thrust it in his arms as he rose to look at her, and turning to the men was gone.

They looked at each other in amazement and disgust. They could hardly believe their senses.

"How dare she do it before us all ? " said one.

CHAPTER XVI.

WAS THE WOMAN INSANE?

AS the boy left the saloon one of the men said, "Now I guess the little cuss will git up and dust." And that thought was their consolation. Not that they hated this boy, but they felt that he was out of place in the cabin of their "Widder."

Other, and equally ingenious ways, all quite as innocent, had been used by the miners to force their gifts upon the one sweet woman, the patron saint of the camp, until she might have been almost as wealthy as the good old saint who lies mouldering before the eyes of all who care to pay a five-franc note, in the mighty cathedral at Milan. But now they would do no more.

Nuggets, and bars, and scales, and specimens, and dust in her home in profusion. And why did the little woman remain in the wilderness? Why did not this little woman rise up some morning, smile a good-bye to those about her, leave the business to Washee-Washee, take her great big bodyguard, mount a mule, turn his head up the corkscrew trail toward the clouds, toward the snow, and find a milder clime?

Who could she have been, this half hermit, this little missionary who had in one winter half civilized, almost christianized, a thousand savage men without preaching a single sermon?

Possibly she knew how rare manhood is where men are thickest, how scarce men are where they stand heaped and huddled up together in millions, and was content to remain with these rough fellows, doing good, receiving their homage.

Possibly there was a point of honor in thus remaining with these men of the mines. It might have been she refused to go away, and leave those behind her in the wilderness to whom she owed all the camp had brought her, because they would have missed her so sadly.

And yet after all had things gone on smoothly there was no great reason for her to hurry away. But as it was, it was certainly going to blow great guns, and she certainly knew it.

But here she was now ill, very ill. All this gold was dross. It was nothing to her now. She could hardly lift her hand to the row of golden oranges that lay there before her on the little mantel. She looked at Sandy as he entered and tried to smile. There were tears in her eyes as she did this, and then she hid her face in her hands.

He went and stood and looked in the fire, and tried to think what he should do. Then he went and stood by her bed, and waited there till she uncovered her face and looked up.

She was very pale, and he tried but could not speak.

"Is it raining, Sandy dear?"

She asked this because as she put her hand out some drops fell down from his head upon her own.

"My pretty baby, my baby in the woods, what in the world is the matter?"

He leaned over her, and his voice trembled as he spoke. Then he went down on his knees, and his beard swept her face.

"Is it cold, Sandy dear? Do you think that we, that I, could cross the mountains to-day? If we went slow and careful, and climbed over the snow on our hands and knees, don't you think it could be done, Sandy?"

She kept on asking this question, and arguing it all the time, because the man kept looking at her in a wild, helpless way, and could not answer a word.

"If we went up the trail a little way at a time, and then rested there under the trees, and waited for the snow to melt, and then went on a little way each day, and so on, as fast as it melted off, up the mountain, do n't you think it could be done, Sandy?"

The man was dumb. He kneeled there, grinding his great palms together, looking all the time, and looking at nothing.

There was a long silence then, and still Sandy kneeled by the bed. His eyes kept wandering about till they lighted on a striped gown that hung hard by on the wall. He fell to counting these stripes. He counted them up and down, and across, and then counted them backward, and was quite certain he had got it all wrong, and fell to counting it over again.

The little woman writhed with pain, and that brought the dreamer to his senses again. It passed, and she, pale, fair, beautiful, with her hair about her like folds of sable fur, she put out her round white arms to the great half-grizzly, half-baby, by her side. She was still a long time then; then she called him pretty names, and she cried as if her heart would break.

"Sandy, I told you it was not best, it was not right, it would not do, that you would be sorry some day, and that you would blame and upbraid me, and that the men would laugh at you and at me. But you would not be put off. Do you not remember how I shut myself up and kept away from you, and would not see you, and how you kept watch, and sent round, and would see me whether or no?"

He now remembered. And what then? Had he repented? On the contrary, he had never loved her half so truly as now. His heart was too full to dare to speak.

"Do you not remember that when I told you all this would happen, that you said it could not happen? That, happen what would, no man should mock or laugh or reprove, and live? Well, now, Sandy dear, it will happen. I have done you wrong. I now want to tell you to take back your promise. That is best."

The man rose up. The place where he had hid his face was wet as rain.

"Sandy, Sandy, can we cross the mountains now?"

The little lady lay trembling in her bed with her hands covering her face.

Then she put down her hands and looked up into the face of her husband.

"Sandy, leave me!"

She sprang up in bed as she said this, as if inspired with a new thought.

"There! take that gold, this gold; all of it!" She left her bed with a bound and heaped the gold together and turned to Sandy.

"Take it, I tell you, and go. That is best;

that is right. I want you to go — go now! Go! Will you go? Will you not go when I command you to go?"

"Not when you 're sick, my pretty; get well, and then I will go; go, and stay till you tell me I may come back."

"Will you not go?"

"Not while you 're sick, my pretty."

"Then I will go."

She caught a shawl from the wall. Her face was aflame. She sprang to the door, through the door, and out to the fence, in a moment. Sandy's arms were about her now, and he led her back and laid her in her bed.

She lay there trembling again, and Sandy bent above her.

"Sandy, when all the world turns against me and laughs at me, what will you do?"

He did not understand; he could not answer.

"When men laugh at me when I pass, what can you say, and what will you do?"

"What will I do?"

The man seemed to hear now, and to understand. He sprang up, spun about, and tossed his head.

"What will I do! Shoot 'em! — scalp every mother's son of 'em!" And he brought his fist down on the little mantel-piece till the bits of gold remaining and the little trinkets leapt half way across the room.

The little woman lay a moment silent, and then she threw back the clothes, and pushing Sandy back, as if he had been a great child, sprang up again, and again dashed through the door.

Limber Tim had been standing there all the time, half hidden behind the fence, against which he had glued his back, waiting to be of some use if possible to the guardian angel of the camp. There was also a row of men reaching within hail all the way down to the town, waiting to be of help, for Limber Tim had told them the Widow was ill.

The man started from his fastening on the fence at sight of this apparition, wild, half-clad, with her hair all down about her loose, ungathered garments, and he stood before her.

"I want to go home," the woman cried, wringing her hands. "I want to go home. I will go home. There is something wrong. You do not understand. Sandy is an angel; I am a devil. I want to go home."

The strong man's arms were about her again as she stood there on the edge of the fence, and he bore her back, half fainting and quite exhausted, into the house.

He laid her down, and stood back as if half

frightened at what he had done. Never before had he put out a finger, said a word, held a thought, contrary to her slightest and most unreasonable whim. Then he came back timidly, as if he was afraid he would frighten her, for she began to tremble again, and she was whiter than before. She did not look up, she was looking straight ahead, down toward her feet, but she knew he was there — knew he would hear her, let her speak never so low.

"When the great trouble comes, Sandy, when the trouble comes and covers both of us with care, will you remember that you would not put me off? When the trouble comes, will you ever remember that you would not let me go away? that you would not go away? Will you remember, Sandy?"

She was getting wild again, and sprang up in bed as she said this last, and looked the man in his face so earnest, so pleading, so pitiful, that Sandy put up his two hands and swore a solemn oath to remember.

She sank back in bed, drew the clothes about her, hid her face from the light, and then Sandy drew back and stood by the fire, and the awful thought came fully and with all its force upon him that she was insane.

Ah! that was what it was. She feared she would go mad. Mad! mad! He thought of all the mad people he had ever seen or heard of; thought how he had been told that it runs in families; how people go mad and murder their friends, destroy themselves, go into the woods and are eaten by wild beasts, lost in the snow, or drowned in the waters hurrying by wood and mountain wall, and then he feared that he should go mad himself.

"Poor little soul!" he kept saying over to himself. "Poor, noble little soul! would not marry me because she knew she would go mad." And she was dearer to the man now than ever before.

"Sandy."

The sufferer barely breathed his name, but he leaned above her while yet she spoke.

"Sandy, bring Billy Piper."

"What?" He threw up his two hands in the air. The woman did not seem to heed him, but, resting and lying quite still a moment, said, softly —

"Bring Bunker Hill."

"Bring what? who?"

"Go, bring Bunker Hill."

If his wife had said, "Bring Satan," or had repeated her "Bring Billy Piper," the man could not have been more surprised or displeased.

Now this Bunker Hill, or Bunkerhill, was a

poor woman of the town — the best one there, it is true, but bad enough, no doubt, at the best. She was called Bunker Hill by the boys, and no one knew her by any other name, because she was a sort of a hunch-back.

"Did you say, my pretty, did you say —"

"Sandy, bring Bunker Hill. And bring her soon. Soon, Sandy, soon; soon, for the love of God."

The woman was writhing with pain again as the man shot through the door, and looked back over his shoulder to be sure that she did not attempt to leave the house or destroy herself the moment his back was turned.

Limber Tim was there waiting silently and patiently. He scratched his head, and wondered, and raised his brim as he ran, and slid, and shuffled with all his speed down the trail toward the town to bring the woman. Men stood by in respectful silence as he passed. They would have given worlds almost to know how the one fair woman fared, but they did not ask the question, did not stop the man a moment. A moment might be precious. It might be worth a life.

There are some rules of etiquette, some principles of feeling in the wild woods among the wild men there, that might be transplanted with advantage to a better society. There might have been a feeling of disappointment or displeasure on the part of the men standing waiting, waiting for an opportunity to be of the least possible service, as they saw Bunker Hill leave town to return with Limber Tim, but it had no expression.

The man who sat behind the silver faro-box no doubt felt this disappointment the keenest of any one.

When we feel displeased or disappointed at any thing, we are always saying that that is about the best that could be done. "What else could she do? The woman's ill; the Widder is sick. She sends for a woman, a bad woman, p'raps, but the best we got. Well, a woman's better as a man, any ways you puts it. What else could she do? A bad woman's better as a good man. What else could she do? I puts it to you, what else could she do?"

The crowd at the Howling Wilderness was satisfied. But the men stood there or sat in knots around the bar-room in silence. The crimson-headed bar-keeper had not seen such a dull day of it since they had the double funeral. What could be the matter? Men made all kinds of guesses, but somehow no one hinted that the little woman was mad.

The Roaring Whirlpool, as the Howling Wilderness was sometimes called, drew in but few victims all that night. Men kept away, kept going out and looking up toward the little cabin on the hill.

The man with the silver faro-box sat by the table with the green cloth, as if in a brown study. The great fire blazed up and snapped as if angry, for but few men gathered about it all that evening. The little brown mice up in the loft could be heard nibbling at the old boots and bacon rinds, and their little teeth ticked and rattled together as if the upper half of the Howling Wilderness had been the shop of a mender of watches. Now and then the man behind the silver faro-box filliped the pack of cards with his fingers, turned up the heels of a jack in the most unexpected sort of way, as if just to keep his hand in, but the mice had it mostly their own way all that night.

One by one the men who stood waiting dropped away and out of the line to get their dinners, but still enough stood there the livelong night to pass a message from mouth to mouth with the speed of a telegram into town.

Then these men standing there, and those who went away, as to that, fell to thinking of Bunker Hill. Somehow, she had advanced wonderfully in the estimation of all from the moment she had been sent for by the Widow. It was a sort of special dignity that had been conferred. This woman, Bunker Hill, had been knighted by their queen. She had been picked out, and set apart and over and above all the other fallen women of the Forks.

Even Limber Tim, who stood there on one leg, with his back screwed tight up against the palings, began to like her overmuch, and to wonder why she also would not make some honest man an honest wife. In fact, many men that night recalled many noble acts on the part of this poor woman, and they almost began to feel ashamed that they had sometimes laughed at her plainness, and promised in their hearts to never do so again.

CHAPTER XVII.

CAPTAIN TOMMY.

THERE was a gray streak of dawn just breaking through the black tree-tops that tossed above the high, far, deep snow, on the mountain that lifted to the east, as the door opened, and Bunker Hill came forth alone. There were ugly clouds rolling overhead, mixing, marching, and counter-marching, as if preparing for a great battle of the elements. On the west wall of the mountain a wolf howled dolefully to his mate on the opposite crest of the cañon. The water tumbled and thundered through the gorge below, and sent up echoes and sounds that were sad and lonesome as the march to the home of the dead.

She came out into the gray day, slowly and thoughtfully, her head was down, and when Limber Tim helped her over the fence she was shy and modest, as if she herself had been the Widow.

He tried to ask about the Widow, but that awful respect for the other sex that seems born with the American of the Far West, kept him silent; and as Bunker Hill led on rapidly towards town and did not say one word about the sufferer, he followed, as ignorant as any man in camp.

On the way the woman slipped on the wet and icy trail and fell, for she was in terrible haste and terribly excited. Perhaps she cut her arm or hand on the sharp stone as she fell, for as she hastily arose and again hurried on, she kept rubbing and holding her right arm with her left.

She led straight to the Howling Wilderness, lifted the latch and entered. She looked all around, but did not speak. She was in a great hurry, and was evidently looking for some one she wished to find at once. No man spoke to her now. The few found there at this hour were the wildest and most reckless in the camp, but they were respectful, as if in the presence of a lady born and bred a lady.

There was something beautiful in this silence and respect. Even the man with the silver faro-box for a breastwork rose up and stood in her presence while she remained. He did not do it on purpose. He would not have done it the day before had she stood before him by the hour. He did not even know when he arose, but when she bowed just the least bit, and turned away and went out again into the cold and did not drink — did not drink, mind you — did not even look at the crimson-headed man who had risen up in perfect confidence, he found himself standing, and found his heart filling with a kind of gallantry that he had not known before. He had risen in her presence by instinct.

"Come, we must find Captain Tommy." The woman said this to Limber Tim as they left the saloon, and then led swiftly on to Captain Tommy's cabin.

This Captain Tommy was a character and a power too, and, wretch as she was, was a woman to be leaned upon, and trusted too to the last.

True, she was very plain. But you may adopt it as one of your rules of life, and act upon it with absolute certainty, that, if you have to trust any woman, trust a plain one, rather than a handsome one; for the plain ones were not made to sell, else they too had been made handsome.

"Not to be too particular about a delicate subject," said old Baldy, who had been fortunate enough to know her, "her memory possibly may reach back to the Black Hawk War."

But the crowning feature of this woman was her enormous head of hair. It was black as night and bushy as a Kanaka's; all about her head in a heap, that seemed to be constantly in motion. But at the back and down between her shoulders it had gathered into a queue, and hung down there like a bell-rope with a black tassel at the end.

She generally kept her mouth closed. But men observed that, when she wanted to say any thing, she pulled up her back, took hold of the bell-rope, and pulled and pulled till her mouth came open; then she would throw out her sunken breast, and wind and wind with her two hands, and corkscrew at her back hair, and pull and twist and wind, until she had wound herself up so tight that it was impossible to close either her mouth or her eyes. After that she could talk faster than any man in the world, and faster than a great many women, until she ran down, and the bell-rope hung loose between her shoulders. Then her mouth would close suddenly, and she would have to stop that instant, even if in the midst of a sentence, until she could seize the bell-rope, pull herself open and wind herself up again.

The Captain had admirers in the Forks; many and many a worshiper, and not altogether without reason. There was about her a certain sweetness of nature that contrasted well with the rough life in which she was thrown; and the strong men noted this, and liked the sense of her presence.

Besides that, this woman had a certain sincerity about her, a virtue that is as rare as it is dear to man. I think, if we look at ourselves clearly, we will discover that this one quality wins upon us more than any other — that is more than beauty, more than gold — sincerity, earnestness. For my part, I only make that one demand on any man or any woman. You can not be graceful at will, or wealthy, or beautiful, or always good-natured; but you can be in earnest. You can refuse to lie, either in word or in deed. I demand that you shall be in earnest before you shall approach me. Be in earnest even in your villainy.

The woman knocked on the door with her knuckles, and called through the hole of the latch-string to the woman within; for Captain Tommy was also a woman, and a woman of the order — of a less order even — than this good Samaritan, who stood calling through the keyhole and shivering with the cold.

There was an answer, and then the two stood there in the bleak, still, cold, gray morning together. There was a noise of somebody dressing in the dark very fast, a hard oath or two, the scratching of a match, the lifting of a latch in the rear of a cabin, the sound of a man's boots scratching over the stones of a back trail that led to the Howling Wilderness, and then the door opened, and Bunker Hill led in instantly, went right up to Captain Tommy, took her hand in her own, and whispered in her ear.

The Captain caught her breath, and then with both hands up, as if to defend herself, staggered close back against the wall. Then, as if suddenly recovering herself, and coming upon a new thought, she relaxed her lifted arms, let them fall, and rounding her shoulders, walked up to the smouldering fire, turned her back, put her hands behind her, looked at Bunker Hill sidewise, and said—

"Yer be darned!"

"It's so, Tommy, sure as gospel, and we want you. She wants you. She sent for you—sent me, and you will come, for you are needed. I can't go it all night. Some people must be there, and that some people must be women."

"No, you don't play me! Go 'long with yer larks! Git!" The Captain was getting out of temper. What was to be done? Bunker Hill went close up to her, and, leaning up, whispered sharply in her ear.

The Captain only said, "Yer be blowed!" and turned and kicked the fire, till it blazed up and filled the room with a rosy light, such only as smouldering pine logs can throw out when roused up into a flame; and then she turned around and looked at Bunker Hill as if she had firmly made up her mind not to be hoaxed. She looked at the good-souled hunch-back before her as if she would look her through; then suddenly her eyes rested on one of her white cuffs. "What the devil's that on yer sleeve? Been in a row again, eh?"

"Come, come, there's no time to lose. It's awful!"

Bunker Hill laid hold of Captain Tommy's arm, and attempted to drag her to the door. She was getting desperate.

Tommy pulled back, and still kept looking at the excited woman's white sleeve or cuff.

"What the devil's that on your sleeve? It looks like blood."

Bunker Hill lifted her arm, looking now herself, pulled back her sleeve, and held it to the light.

"Blood it is! Will you believe me now?"

The stubborn woman, who had been standing on the defensive, with her back to the fire, darted forward now all excitement, all sympathy. She snatched her outer garments from the foot of the bed, where they had lain all this interview, and threw them on her back. She did not stop to fasten them. She caught a blanket from the bed, threw it over her head, as she passed out all breathless, and left the cabin-door wide open, with the fitful pine fire making ghosts on the floor, and the fitful March morning riding in on the wind and sowing it with ashes.

CHAPTER XVIII.

"BLOOD!"

LIMBER TIM all this time had held his back against the wall as firmly as if it was about to fall on all their heads, and their lives depended on his strength. His mouth had been wide open with wonder. He had not understood at all from the first, but now he was more than bewildered — he was terrified.

Blood! blood! He unscrewed himself from the wall, went, winding his long limber legs up the trail, past the Howling Wilderness, after the silent but excited women; and all the time this awful sentence of Bunker Hill's was shooting through his brain—"Blood! blood! it is! Will you believe me now?"

He reached his post by the pine fence, and, being no wiser than before, he again wound himself up against the palings, and reached back his arms and wove them through the pickets, and stood there on one leg looking over his shoulder as the two women disappeared into the Widow's cabin.

Dawn comes slowly down in these dark, deep, wooded cañons of the Sierras. Morning seems to be battling with the night. Night is entrenched in the woods, and retreats only by inches — the Battle of the Wilderness.

In the steel-gray dawn, cold and sharp, Limber Tim heard a cry that knocked him loose from the fence. He picked himself together, and again twisted himself into the pickets; but all the time he kept seeing Bunker Hill pushing back her sleeve, holding up her arm in the ghostly light of the pine-log fire, and saying, "Blood it is! Will you believe me now?"

"Blood," mused the man. "Somebody's hurt. Somebody's hurt awful bad, too, or they would n't keep a feller a-standin' agin a fence the whole blessed night."

The man's teeth began to chatter. The thought of blood and the bleak cold morning kept them smiting together as if he had had an ague.

A man in great gum boots came screeching by the cabin; his nose was pointed straight for the Howling Wilderness, but backing against Limber Tim as he hung up against the fence, stopped, and asked timidly and very respectfully of the Widow.

Limber held his head thoughtfully to one side, as if he was trying to balance the important facts in his mind, and reveal only just so much of the condition of the Widow, or Sandy, or Bunker Hill, or whoever it was that was hurt, as was best, and no more, but for a time was silent.

A thought struck him, and he mused: Sandy's cut his foot, or p'raps it 's Bunker Hill shot herself with that darned pistol she allers packs in her breeches' pocket.

"Well, an' 'ow 's the Widder?" The man was getting impatient for his drink.

"It ain't the Widder at all. It 's Sandy. Sandy's cut his foot — cut his foot last night a cuttin' wood in the dark. That 's what 's the matter."

Limber Tim pecked his head, pursed up his mouth, and for the first time in his life, perhaps, felt that he was really a man of some consequence.

"By the holy poker! thought it was the Widder."

"Not much. It 's Sandy. Cut his foot, I tell yer. Blood clean up to his elbows. Blood all over the house. Bunker Hill all over blood. Hell 's a poppin', I tell yer." And poor Limber Tim so excited himself by this recital, that he broke loose from the fence, and chattered his teeth together like a chipmunk with a hazel-nut.

Then the man passed on down the trail, and

Limber Tim again grew on to the fence, and chattered his teeth together, and waited developments, not at all certain that he had not lied.

"'Ow 's the Widder, Limber?"

Limber unloosed himself from the fence, and tried to stand straight up and tell the truth and nothing but the truth.

"Better, thank yer. That is, the blood is stopped, or most of it, you know — the most of it. Bunker Hill is hurt some too, you know. Blood all over her arm. Poor girl, poor girl! but she did n't whimper. Not she. Nary a sniff."

"Both of 'em hurt?"

"Yes, same bullet, you know — same shot — same pistol — same —"

The man had too much to tell already, and almost ran in his haste to reach the Howling Wilderness and tell what had happened.

This time, as Limber Tim screwed himself up against the fence, he felt pretty certain that somewhere or somehow during the morning he had lied like a trooper, and was very miserable.

"Hard on Sandy that," said the bar-keeper to the second early-riser, who had just arrived, as he stood behind his breastwork in his night-shirt, and handed down to his customer his morning bottle, with his hairy arms all naked, and his red uncombed hair reaching up like the blaze from a pine-knot fire.

"Yes," answered the man, as he fired a volley down his throat, and then fell back to the fire, wiping his big bearded mouth with the back of his hand, "Yes, but Limber Tim says she 'll soon be up again; says the blood 's all stopped, and all that. You see, the signs are all in her favor. It 's a good thing for a shot, to see it bleed. Best thing for a bad shot is to see it bleed well. That is, if yer can stop the blood in time. But now, in this 'ere case, the blood 's all stopped. Just come down from there. Limber just told me blood 's all stopped."

There was a man standing back in the corner by the fire, half in the dark, warming the lower end of his back and listening with both ears all this time. He now came out of the dark, and began —

"You darned infernal fool! Sold clean out. It 's not the Widder at all — it 's Sandy. Split his foot open with an ax. Blood gushed out all over Bunker Hill. Kivered Bunker Hill with blood clean up to the elbows."

"And what the devil was Bunker Hill a-doin' at Sandy's?"

The man from the dark saw that somebody had been sold, and, fearing it might possibly be himself, simply pecked at the other man, staggered up to the bar, pecked at the head that blazed like a pine-knot fire, and then the three drank in silence. There was a sort of truce, a silent but well-understood agreement, that nothing further should be said, but that, when the truth came out, one should not tell on the other, and turn the laugh of the camp upon him.

Early the men began to drop in to the Great Whirlpool, the one great center of this snow-walled world, to ask gently, and with tender concern in their faces, after the fortunes of the Widow.

It was a great day for the cinnamon-haired little man, and he made the most of it. Men fell into disputes the moment they arrived, but, as no one knew any thing, they always settled it with a treat all round, and then waited for results.

The bar-keeper was appealed to, as bar-keepers, like barbers, are supposed to know all the news. But this man, like most bar-keepers in the wilderness, was a cautious man, and said he knew all about it, but could not take sides or decide between his friends. Time would tell who was right and who was wrong.

At last the Judge rolled in like a little sea on the shore. He had come straight down from the Widow's, had gone up to get the truth of the matter, and had unscrewed Limber Tim from the fence, and made him tell all he knew of the unhappy lady, and how it happened.

Then the boys backed the little Judge up against the bar, and stood him there, and read him from top to bottom, as if he had been a bulletin board.

"Split his foot clean open, you see! Did it while a choppin' wood in the dark."

"Speck he was a lookin' at the Widder when it happened," half laughed a big man with a big mouth, and a voice like a Numidian lion.

"The clumsy cuss!"

That is what Oregon Jake said after catching his breath over his tumbler of Old Tom. And that is all the sympathy that Sandy got after they found out, as they thought, that he had only split open his foot with an ax.

"The clumsy cuss!"

CHAPTER XIX.

HOW DID IT HAPPEN?

THE sun at last shot sharply through the far fir tops tossing over the savage and sublime mountain crest away to the east, with its battlement of snow, and Limber Tim was glad at the sight of it, for he was very cold and stiff, and hungry and thirsty, and tired of his post of honor, and disgusted with himself for the miserable mistakes he had made that morning.

He had been standing there like a forlorn and lonesome cock all the morning on one foot, waiting for the dawn, and now he fairly wanted to crow at the sight of it.

Men came and went now, and every man asked after poor Sandy.

Limber Tim now told the same story right straight through, all about how it happened, how Bunker Hill was "kivered" with blood, and all about it, even to the most minute detail; for certainly, thought he to himself, it is Sandy or Sandy would have come out long ago. He even believed it so firmly, that he began to be sorry for Sandy, and to wonder how long it would be till Sandy would be out and about again on crutches. Then he said to himself, it would be at least a month; and then when the next man came by and inquired after Sandy, he told him that in a month Sandy would be about on crutches. At this piece of information Limber Tim felt a great deal better. He said to himself he was very glad it was no worse, and then he screwed his back tighter up to the fence than before, and stood there trying to warm in the cold sunlight of a moist morning in the Sierras. It was like standing on the Apennines, and turning your back and parting your coat tails, and trying to warm by the fires of Vesuvius.

In the midst of meditations like these the door opened, and Sandy shuffled through it, shot over the fence, slapped his two great hands on the two shoulders as before, and before Limber Tim could unscrew himself from the fence, cried out —

"Whisky, Limber! whisky, quick! The gals is almost tuckered! Go! Split!"

He spun him around and sent him reeling down the trail, then returned and banged the door behind him.

Limber Tim scratched his ear as he stumbled over the rocks in the trail, and wound his stiffened legs about the boulders and over the logs on his way to the Howling Wilderness, and was sorely perplexed.

"Wal, it ain't Sandy, any way. Ef his big hands have lost any of their grip I do n't see it, anyhow." He shrugged his shoulders as he said this to himself, for they still ached from the vice-like grip of the giant.

Still Limber Tim was angry, notwithstanding the discovery that his old partner was sound and well, and he lifted the latch with but one resolution, and that was to remain perfectly silent and let his lies take care of themselves.

Men crowded around him as he entered and gave his orders. But this bulletin-board was a blank. He had set his lips together and they kept their place. For the first time in his troubled and shaky existence he began to know and to feel the power and the dignity of silence. He knew that every man there thought that he, who stood next to the throne, knew all; and felt dignified by this, and dared even to look a little severe on those who were about to ask him questions.

He had crammed a bottle of so-called "Bourbon" in his left boot, and was just pushing into the right a "phial of wrath," when some one in the cabin sighed, "Poor Sandy!"

Still Limber Tim went on pushing the phial

of wrath into his gum boot as well as he could with his stiffened fingers.

Then a man came up sharply out of the crowd, and throwing a big, heavy bag of gold dust, as fat as a pet squirrel, down on the counter, proposed to raise a "puss" for Sandy.

This was too much. Limber Tim raised his head, and slipping as fast as he could through the crowd for the door, said, back over his shoulder —

"It ain't Sandy at all. It's Bunker Hill. It's the gals. The gals is almost tuckered."

There was the confusion of Babel in the Howling Wilderness. The strange and contradictory accounts that had come down from the Widow's — their shrine, the little log house that to them was as a temple, a city set upon a hill—were anything but satisfactory. The men began to get nervous, and then they began to drink, and then they began to dispute again, and then they began to bet high and recklessly who it was that had cut his foot.

"Got it all right now," said poor Limber Tim to himself as he made his way up the trail as fast as possible, with the two bottles in the legs of his great gum boots for safe carriage. "Got it all right now! That's it. Bunker Hill cut her foot or shot her hand with that darned derringer, or something of the kind. That's it, that 's where the blood came from, that 's why she 's tuckered — that 's what 's the matter." And so saying and musing to himself, he reached his post, uncorked the phial of wrath, as it was called, looked in at the contents, turned it up towards the sun as if it had been a sort of telescope, and smacking his lips felt slightly confirmed in his opinion. He also resolved to ask Sandy, like a man, what the devil was up the moment he appeared.

Again the door flew open, Sandy flew out, rushed over the fence, took the Bourbon from the trembling hand of Limber Tim, and before he could get his wits together had disappeared and banged the door behind him.

Limber Tim did not like this silent-dignity business a bit. "Lookee here!" he said, as he again turned the telescope up to the sun, and then looked at the door, "I 'll see what 's what, I reckon."

He went up to the fence, leaned over, but his heart failed him.

Then he resorted to the phial of wrath, again looked at the sun, and as he replaced it in his boot felt bold as a lion. The man was drunk. He climbed the fence, staggered up to the door, lifted the latch and pushed it open.

Bunker Hill came softly out of the bed-room, pushed the man back gently as if he had been a child, shut the door slowly, and the man went back to his post.

Men have curiosity as well as women. Weak women over weaker tea, discussing strong scandal in some little would-be-fashionable shoddy saloon in Paris, are not more curious than were these half-wild men here in the woods. The difference however is, this was an honest sympathetic interest. It was all these men had outside of hard work to interest them. They wanted to know what was the matter in their little temple on the hill. The camp was getting wild.

Limber Tim tried to screw himself up against the fence for some time, and failing in this, turned his attention again to the phial of wrath. He was leaning over, trying to get it out of his boot leg, when the door opened and Bunker Hill stepped out carefully, but supple and straight as he had ever seen her.

Limber Tim was quite overcome. He looked up the cañon and then down the cañon.

"They 'll be a comet next." He shook his head hopelessly at this remark of his, and again bent down and wrestled with the boot leg and bottle.

"Bully for Bunker Hill. Guess she 's not hurt much after all."

The men went out of the Howling Wilderness as the man who shot this injunction or observation in at the door went in, and to their amazement saw the woman alluded to walk rapidly on past the saloon. She did not look up, she did not turn right or left or stop at the saloon or speak to any one; she went straight to her own cabin. Then the men knew for a certainty that it was the little Widow who was ill, and they knew that it was this woman who was nursing her, and they almost worshiped the ground that the good Samaritan walked upon.

Soon Bunker Hill came out again, and again took the trail for the Widow's cabin, and walking all the time rapidly as before. The men as she passed took off their hats and stood there in silence.

There was a smile of satisfaction on her plain face as she climbed the hill. She went up that hill as if she had been borne on wings. Her heart had never been so light before. For the first time since she had been in camp, she had noticed that she was treated with respect. It was a rare sensation, new and most delightful. The hump on her back was barely noticed as she passed Limber Tim trying to lean up against the fence, and entered with a noiseless step, and almost tip-toe, the home of the sufferer.

The men respected this woman now more than ever before. They also respected her silence.

At another time they would have called out to her; sent banter after her in rough unhewn speech, and got in return as good, or better, than they sent. But now no man spoke to her. She had been dignified, sanctified, by her mission of mercy, whatever it meant or whatever was the matter, and she was to them a better woman. Men who met her on her return gave her all the trail, and held their hats as she passed. One old man gave her his hand as she crossed a little snow stream in the trail, and helped her over it as if she had been his own child. Yet this old man had despised her and all her kind the day before.

She went and came many times that day, and always with the same respect, the same silent regard from the great Missourians whom the day found about the Forks.

Then Captain Tommy came forth in the evening, and also went on straight to her cabin, and her face was full of concern. The Captain had not been a person of any dignity at all the day before, but now not a man had the audacity to address her as she passed on with her eyes fixed on the trail before her.

When she returned, the man at his post had fallen. Poor Limber Tim! He would not leave his station, and Sandy had something else to think of now; and so he fell on the field.

It was not that he had drunk so much, but that that he had eaten so little. His last recollections of that day were a long and protracted and fruitless wrestle with the phial of wrath in his boot-leg, and an ineffectual attempt to screw the picket fence on to his back.

It was no new thing to find a man spilt out in the trail in these days, and his fall excited no remark.

They would carry men in out of the night and away from the wolves, or else would sit down and camp by them till they were able to care for themselves.

A man took a leg under each arm, another man took hold of his shoulders, and Limber Tim, now the limpest thing dead or alive was borne to his cabin.

One — two — three days. The camp, that at first was excited almost beyond bounds, had gone back to its work, and only now and then sent up a man from the mines below, or sent down a man from the mines above, to inquire if there was yet any news from the Widow. But not a word was to be heard.

All these days the two women went and came right through the thick of the men, but no man there was found rude enough to ask a question.

Never had the camp been so sober. Never

had the Forks been so thoughtful. The cinnamon-headed bar-keeper leaned over his bar and said confidentially to the man at the table behind the silver faro-box, who had just awakened from a long nap

"Ef this 'ere thing keps up, I busts." Then the red-haired man drew a cork and went on a protracted spree all by himself.

"Send for a gospel sharp all to once, Jake. Let 's go the whole hog. The Forks only wants to get religion now, and die."

CHAPTER XX.

A FLAG OF TRUCE.

HOW beautiful was all this profound veneration for woman in this wild Eden! How high and holy the influence of this one woman over these half-grizzlies, these hairy-faced men who had drunk water from the same spring with the wild beasts of the Sierras.

Now they would not drink, would hardly shout or speak sharp, while she lay ill. Whatever was the matter, or the misfortune, they had too much respect for her, for themselves, to carouse till she should again show her face, or at least while her life was uncertain.

The fourth day came down into the cañon, and sat down there as a sort of pioneer Summer. Birds flew over the camp from one mountain side to the other, and sang as they flew. Men whistled old tunes in a dreamy sort of a way as they came up from their work that day, and recalled other days, and were boys once more in imagination, away in the world that lay beyond the Rocky Mountains.

"There is something in this glorious climate of Californy, say what you will," mused the Judge, as he lit his pipe and sat down on a stump in the street.

Limber Tim and the cinnamon-haired man had settled down into that collapse which always follows a protracted spree or a heavy carouse, and they too sat on their respective stumps out in the open air, while the saloon was left all to the little brown mice upstairs.

Men were lounging all up and down the street on old knotty logs that no ax could reduce to firewood, or leaning against the cabins on the warm sides that were still warm with the sunshine gone away, or loafing up and down with their pipes in their mouths, and their ragged coats thrown over one shoulder, like the bravos of Italy. Certainly there was something in the glorious climate of California.

There had been no news from the Widow all this time.

A keen-eyed man just now lifted his eyes in the direction of the cabin. In fact, it was a custom—an instinct, to lift the face in that direction many times a day. If any of these men ever prayed in that camp, and the truth could be told, you would find that that man first turned the face and kneeled looking in that direction. Her house was a sort of second Mecca.

The camp, however, after being a long time patient and silent, had got a little cross. Yet it had not lost a bit of its blunt and honest manhood. It had simply made up its mind that the Widow and Sandy were both of age, and able to take care of themselves. If they were willing to get the toothache, or something of the kind, and then retreat into their cabin, and pull the latch-string inside after them, they could do so, and the camp would not interfere.

The man who had been looking up the hill now turned to his partner, drew his pipe from his mouth, wrinkled up his brows, and then slowly reached out his arm and with his pipe-stem pointed inquiringly up the hill.

A man and a woman were coming slowly and cautiously down the way from the Widow's cabin. They were coming straight for the great center of the Forks, the Howling Wilderness.

The woman had something in her arms. She walked as carefully as if she had been bearing a waiter of wine. Could this be the Widow? It could hardly be Bunker Hill, thought the Forks, as it rose up from its seat on the stumps, and lifted its face up the trail, for she is almost as tall and comely and steps as nimbly as any woman in camp.

Could this be Sandy? He looked larger than ever before — a sort of Gog or Magog.

The man stuck his pipe between his teeth again and puffed furiously for a minute, and then sat down over the log again, let his feet dangle in the air, and, leaning forward, rocked to and fro as if nursing his stomach, and seemed wrapped in thought.

"Sandy, by the great Cæsar!"

"Bunker Hill, by the holy poker!"

"And what 's that she got a carryin'?"

"It 's a table-cloth a hangin' out for dinner!"

"It 's a flag of truce!" cried the Judge, standing on tip-toe on his stump and straightening his fat little body up towards the Sierras.

"And has n't Sandy grow'd since we seed 'im, eh!"

"And do n't he step high! Jerusalem, do n't he step high!"

"And where 's Captain Tommy, and where 's the Widow?" anxiously inquired the Forks, still looking up the hill towards its little shrine.

At last they entered the town, and the town met them on the edge—at its outer gate, as it were, with all its force.

The woman indeed bore a flag of truce. A long white banner streamed from her arms and fell down to her feet, and almost touched the ground. A close observer would have seen that this flag was made of the very same coarse material from which the Widow had made the curtains of her little bed.

They entered the edge of the town, these three, and the town stood there as silent as if it had risen up on its way to church on a Sunday morning. These three, do you mind, stood there still, right in the track of the town, and the town looking at them as if they had come from another world. And so at least they had, a part of them.

These three: Sandy, Bunker Hill, and the first baby born in the mines of the Sierras.

Bunker Hill held the baby out in one hand, and with the other tenderly lifted back the covering, while Sandy stood by like a tower on a hill, smiling, pushing back his hat, pulling down his whiskers, looking over the little army of men with a splendid sort of sympathy and self-accusation combined. He seemed to be saying, as he turned their eyes to the little red half opened rose-bud, "Just look there! see what I 've done." His great face was radiant with delight.

And then there was a shout—such a shout! The spotted clouds that blew about the tall pine tops, indolent and away up on the mountain's brow, seemed to be set in motion again; the coyote rose up from his sleep on the mountain side and called out to his companions across the gorge as if he had been frightened; while Captain Tommy, who had been left with the Widow, came to the door and stood there, listening and looking down into the camp to see what in the world had happened. She saw men's hats go up in the air, and then again the shouts shook the town.

"Three cheers for Sandy!" They were given with a tiger. "Three cheers for the Widow! three cheers for Missus Bunker Hill." And then the poor girl leaning out of the door, took up her apron and wiped tears of joy from her eyes, for "three times three" were given for Captain Tommy. Then she went back into the house, back to the bed-room with the curious little curtains and gunny-bag carpets, and told the Widow, and the two women wept in each other's arms together.

Men slapped each other on the back, bantered each other, and talked loud of old Missouri and the institution of marriage.

Of all things perhaps this baby was the last they had looked for or thought of. In a camp of thousands, where the youngest baby there, save the boy poet, had a beard on his face, the men had forgotten to think of children. It is quite likely they fancied that children would not grow in the Sierras at all.

The Judge was the first to come forward as

was his custom. He looked it in the face, began to make a speech, but only could say, "It 's this glorious climate of Californy." And then he blushed to the tip of his nose, backed out, and others came in turn to see the wonderful little creature that had come all alone, farther than across the plains, farther than any of them, farther than the farthest of the States, even from the other world, to settle in the Sierras.

"Well ef that ain 't the littlest!"

"Is that all the big they is?"

"Well! do n't think Sandy hardly got his first planting, did he, Pike?"

"Well, that bangs me all hollow!"

"Dang my cats if it 's bigger nor my thumb!"

"Devil of a little thing to make such a big row about, eh?"

Sandy was all submission and pride and tenderness, and received the congratulations and heard the good-humored speeches of the good-humored men as if they were all meant in compliment to him.

How radiant and even half beautiful was the plain face of poor Miss Bunker Hill as she lifted it up before the camp now, conscious that she had done a good thing and had a right to look the world in the face, and receive its kindness and encouragement.

Older men and more thoughtful came up at last, to look upon the little wonder and to read the story of this new volume fresh from the press. They looked long and silently. They were as gentle as lambs. Death had no terror to them, it was not half so solemn, so mysterious, as this birth in the heart of the Sierras. Life was there, then, as well as death. People would come and go there as elsewhere. The hand of God had stretched over the mountain, down into the awful gorge, and set down a little angel at their cabin doors. It was very, very welcome, and the old men bobbed their heads with delight.

At last all was still, and the little Judge felt that this was not an occasion to be lost. In fact, had there been a clergyman there to say a word, it had had more good effect than all the funeral sermons that the little red-faced man had pronounced in the camp. The occasion was a singular one, and the men's hearts were now as mellow as new-plowed land that had long lain fallow and waiting for the seed.

"This, my friends," began the little man, standing upon a stump, and extending his hands towards the baby, "this, my friends, shows us that the wonderful climate of Californy—" Just then some one poked the fat little fellow in the stomach with his pipe-stem, and he doubled up like a jack-knife and quietly got down, as if nothing had happened.

There was a lull then, and things began to look embarrassing. Sandy was now of course too proud, too happy, too much of a man to carouse, but he called the cinnamon-headed man to his side by a crook of his finger, and making the sign so well known in the Sierras, and so well understood by all who are thirsty, the parties divided — the camp to carouse to the little stranger in the Howling Wilderness, and Sandy to return to his "fam'ly."

"Here's to—to—to—here's to it! Here's to the Little Half-a-pint!" The men were standing in a row, their glasses high up, and dipping in every angle and to every point of the compass, but they did not know the baby's name; they did not even know its sex. And so in that moment, without stopping to think, and without any time to spare, they spoke of it as "it," and they named it Little Half-a-pint.

CHAPTER XXI.

THE QUESTION NONE COULD ANSWER.

HOW the Widow's heart had been beating all this time! How she waited, and waited, and listened, and how often she sent Captain Tommy to the door to tell her, if possible, how her baby fared among the half-wild men of the camp.

How glad she was when she saw Sandy enter, all flurry and delight, as if he had been the central figure in some great triumph. Then a bit of the old sadness and cast of care swept over her face, and she nestled down in the pillow and put up her two hands to hide a moment from the light.

The other two were too busy with the little Half-a-pint to notice her trouble then. They laid it down in a cradle that had been made for rocking and washing gold, and good little Bunker Hill sat by it, and crossed her legs and took up her work, and went on sewing and singing to herself, and swinging her leg that hung over, and rocking the cradle with her foot in the old fashioned way when babies were born in the leaves of the woods of the Wabash, and mothers sat singing by the camp-fires, knitting and rocking their babies in their sugar-troughs.

Down in the Howling Wilderness I am bound to say the carousing began early, and with a vigor that promised more headaches than the camp had known since the Widow first set foot in the Forks.

Little Half-a-pint was toasted and talked of in every corner of the house. Was it a girl or was it a boy? Why had they not asked so simple and so civil a question? They called for Limber Tim — they would appeal to him. But Limber Tim was not to be found in all the manifold depths of the Howling Wilderness. He had had his carouse, and was now playing sober Indian. In fact, he was hanging very close about the little rocking cradle up in the front room of the Widow's cabin. Never was the cradle allowed to rest, but rock, rock, till the Widow and Sandy too were both made very sensible, sleeping or waking, that little Half-a-pint, small as it was, was filling up the biggest half of the house.

Nearly midnight it was when Limber Tim, leaning over the cradle and looking, or pretending to look, at the baby, said to Bunker Hill, who bent down over it on the other side, "Pretty, ain't it?"

"Guess it is. Looks just like its father for the world." And little hump-backed Bunker Hill began to make faces, and to shake her head and nod it up and down, and coo and crow to little Half-a-pint as if it was really able to hear, and understand, and answer all she said to it.

Down at the saloon all this time the spirits flowed like water. The cinnamon-haired fellow had fallen upon a harvest, and was making the most of it. He had laid off his coat, run his two hands up through his hair till it stood up like forked flames, and was thumping the glasses as if in feats of legerdemain. How he did score with the charcoal on the hewn logs behind. He marked and scored that night till the wall behind him looked as if it might be the Iliad written in Greek, or all the characters on the obelisk of Saint Peter's.

Yet with all this happiness on the hill, and this merry-making under the hill, in the heart of the Sierras, in commemoration and celebration of the beginning of a new race in a new land, there was one man back in the corner of the saloon who looked on with something of a sneer on his hard, hatchet face, and who refused to take any part. Now and then this man would lift up his left hand, hold out his fingers and count, one, two, three, four, five, to himself with his other hand, and then shake his head.

The men began to look at him and wonder what he meant. Then this man would count again — one, two, three, four, five, six, seven. Then, when the men would waddle by in their great gum-boots and look back at him over their beards, he would look them square in the face and wink, and screw and shrug his shoulders.

This man stopped there in the middle of the spree, and pursing his brow, and holding up his fingers once more, and looking as profound as if wrestling with a problem in Euclid, said to himself: "Hosses is ten, cows is six, cats is three; but human bein's? Blowed if I know." And he shook his head.

At last this hard, hatchet-faced looking man, standing back alone in the corner, seemed to have got it all counted up to his own satisfaction. He counted, however, again; then he said, as if to himself, "Seven months at the very outside," and slapped his hands together with great glee, and sucked his thin brown lips as if he had just tasted something very delicious.

Then this hatchet-faced fellow, still rubbing his hands and still twirling his lip, and all the time grinning with a grin that was sweet and devilish, turned to the first man at his side, and whispered in his ear.

This man started and spun around when the hard-faced man had finished as if he had been a top, and the hatchet-faced fellow had struck him with a whip.

The man spun about, in fact, till the hard-faced fellow caught hold of his eye with his own and held him there till he could catch his breath. Then the man, after catching his breath, and catching it again, said slowly, but most emphatically:

"Ompossible!"

The hatchet-faced man simply pecked in the face of the other. He did not say any thing more to him, but he pecked at him again, and he pecked emphatically, too, and in a way that would not admit of any two opinions; as if the man were a grain of corn, and he had half a mind to pick him up and swallow him down for daring to hint that it was impossible.

Then the man went off suddenly to one side, and he too fell to counting on his fingers, and to taking a whole knot of men into his confidence.

Then the hatchet-faced fellow went up to another man and whispered in his ear, with his smirk and his sweet devilish smile, and he soon set him to spinning round like a top, and to lifting up his fingers and counting one, two, three, four, five.

Then all around the saloon men began to get sober and to hold up their hands and to count their fingers.

At last the little fat red-faced Judge was heard to say —

"They was married in the Fall."

"About — about — about — eh, about what month, do you remember, eh?" squeaked out the hatchet-faced interrogation point through the nose, as he planted himself before the little Judge.

"About the last cleaning up," said the Judge cheerfully.

"That was about — about—" and the hatchet-faced man with the nasal twang and sharp nose began again to count on his fingers — "about four, five, six, seven months ago?"

"Yes, yes," said the good-natured, unsuspicious, important little Judge, "about six, seven months ago, I reckon." And then he, smiling innocently, fell in between two great bearded giants, as a sort of ham-sandwich filling, to take a drink at the bar.

"Ompossible!" said the first top to the hatchet-face.

"Ask him."

The hatchet-face and sharp-nose looked towards the little fat Judge wedged in between the giants. The top spun up to the little Judge, wedged his head in between the giants' shoulders, and asked a question.

The Judge shook his head, and then wiping his mouth with the back of his hand, said half sadly, "No, I am not. No, I am sorry to say, I am not. That is a happiness still in store. No, I am not a family man. Never was married in my life; but whatever may transpire in this glorious climate of Californy —"

The top had its answer, and spun back to its place without waiting for the last of the speech.

The two men talked together again. Then they appealed to an old man who sat mute and sullen back on the bench by the bulldog.

"No, he didn't know about such things; didn't care a cuss anyhow." And the two men went away as if a flea or two had left the dog and hopped into their ears. They went to another man. "Don't see the point, blowed ef I do. Six months, seven months, eight months, ten months, all along there, I 'spose. The great Washington, Cæsar, Horace Greeley, all sich big-bugs, it might take one, two, three years. That little cuss to-day only a month or two, I reckon. It's all right, I reckon. It ain't my funeral, any how. And what the devil you come botherin' of me for, anyhow? Ef yer don't want to drink yerself, let a fellow alone what does!" And he shook them off with a gesture of the hand and a jerk of the head that meant a great deal more than he had said.

There were not so many fingers up now as before. The question evidently had been settled in the minds of the men fully in favor of the little Half-a-pint. Few understood these things at all, fewer still cared to go into particulars at this time, and the question would keep till they had more leisure and less whisky.

Finally, the hatchet-faced man went round and sat down opposite the man who sat behind the little silver faro-box by the pine-table, and began to whisper in his ear. The good-natured genius, half-gambler, half-miner, who had played the little prank with the salmon and gold-dust, had had a dull night of it, and most like even for that reason was a little out of humor. At all events he did not answer at once, but set down his little silver box, and, taking up his cards, began to spin them one by one over the heads of the men, or through the crowd as it opened, back at the old bull-dog that lay on the bunk on the bags of gold under the blankets, and half whistling to himself as he did so.

The hatchet-faced man, fearing the man had forgotten his presence and his revelation, leaned over again and began to whisper and to count on his fingers.

Then he looked sharp at the gambler and began again; "Hits my 'pinion that it's that boy, Billie Piper."

"How many months did you say?" asked the gambler at last.

"Seven or eight at the furthest."

"And how many had it ought to be?"

"Twelve!" And the smile that was sweet and devilish played about the thin blue lips below the sharp and meddlesome nose.

"And are you a family man?"

"No."

"And you say she's bilked us?"

"Yes."

"You're a darn'd infernal liar!" The gambler rose as he said this, snatched up his silver box and dashed it into the teeth of Hatchet-face. And he, coward as he was, put up his hands and held them to his mouth while the blood ran down between his fingers.

"I do n't keer, Judge, I do n't keer, if I broke every tooth in his head. I do n't 'low no white-livered son of a gun to go about a-talking about a woman like that."

Then the gambler, walking off, said to those around him in a lower tone, "It do n't take no twelve months nohow. Now there's the yaller cat; 'bout four litters in a year. Twelve months be blowed! That's an old woman's story. Then that's in Missoury, anyhow, and what's the climate of Missoury got to do with Californy, I'd like to know? No, gentlemen; some apples gits ripe soon, and some do n't git ripe till frost comes. Them's things, gentlemen, as we do n't know nothing about. Them's mysteries, and none of our business, nohow. Show me the man," and here he began to roar like a Numidian lion, and to tower up above the crowd, while a face like a razor shot out through the door, looking back frightened as it fled, "Show me the man as says it's not all right, and I'll shake him out of his boots."

The gambler picked up his battered box, but he was evidently not in a good humor. He wiped it on his coat-sleeve, and polished it up and down, but was ill content. At last, looking out from under his great slouch hat, he saw the top in the center of a little knot of men holding up his hand and counting his fingers. He threw the box down on the table and rushed into the knot of men.

"A bully set you are, ain't you? Gw'yne around a-counting up after a sick woman. And what do you know, anyhow?" He took hold of the nervous top, and again set it spinning. "That little woman, she come as we come.

God Almighty did n't set no mark and gauge on you, and you shan't go 'round and count up after her. Do you hear? Now you git. You 're wanted. Hatchet-face wants yer. Do you hear?"

The man spun his top about till its face was to the door, and it went out as a sort of handle to the hatchet, and was seen no more that night.

Yet for all this there had been a great ripple in the wave that had to run even to the shore before it could disappear from the face of things at the Forks.

CHAPTER XXII.

DEBATABLE GROUND.

THE next day when Sandy came down, the enthusiasm was at a low ebb. He missed the great reception he had expected, and went back home that night a troubled and anxious man.

What could be the matter? He asked Limber Tim, but Limber Tim had learned the power and security of silence, and either could not or would not venture on any revelations. Besides that, he was very busy helping Bunker Hill with the baby. The camp openly and at all convenient times discussed the question now, and it began to gradually take shape in the minds of men that something was really wrong. Kind old Sandy did not dream what the trouble could be. He feared he had not been generous enough under his good fortune, and was all the time opening the mouth of his leather bag at the bar and pouring gold dust into the scales, and entreating the boys to drink to the health of their little Half-a-pint.

"Yes, our little Half-a-pint it is, I reckons; leastwise it 's pretty certain it ain't yourn." Sandy looked at the man, and then the man set down his glass untouched and went off. He had not meant all that he had said, but having blurted it out in a very awkward way and at the very worst time, got off and out of it as best he could.

Sandy was tortured. The dear little Widow saw it, and asked him what the trouble was, and the man, blunt, honest fellow, told all that had happened.

The camp was disgusted with the man who had mooted this question. They counted him a traitor to the Forks — a sort of Judas. If he had gone and hung himself the camp would have been perfectly satisfied. In fact, it is pretty certain that the camp would have been very glad to have had any excuse, even the least bit of an excuse, to do that office for him.

Then the camp was angry with Sandy, too, on general principles. He had betrayed them into a sort of idol-worship under a mistake. He had lured it into the expression of an enthusiasm quite out of keeping with the dignity of a rough and hardy race of men, and it did not like it.

"The great big idiot!" said the camp. "Did n't he know any better? Do n't he know any better now than to go on in this way half-tickled to death, thinking himself the happiest and the most blest of men?" The camp was ashamed of him.

The little Judge, finding things going against the first family of the Forks, felt also that he in some way was concerned, and felt called upon to explain. This was his theory and explanation.

"The Widow was a widow?"

"Yes."

"The Legislature met at San José on the first day of September?"

"Yes."

"The Legislature granted that first session enough divorces to fill a book?"

"Well?"

"This young woman, this Widow, might 'a bin married; she might 'a bin on her way to the mountains; she might 'a stopped in there and got her divorce, one day on her way up; she might 'a come right on here and got coaxed into marrying Sandy."

"Rather quick work, would n't it be, Judge?"

"Well, considering the climate of Californy, I think not." And the little man pushed out his legs under the card-table, puffed out his little red cheeks, leaned back, and felt perfectly certain that he had made a great point, while the wise men of the camp sat there more confused than before.

However, as the days went by men went on with their work in their mines down in the boiling, foaming, full little streams, now overflowing from the snows that melted in the warm Spring sun, and said but little more on the subject. It was certain that they were very doubtful, for they only shook their heads as a rule when the subject was mentioned now in the great center. That was a bad sign, and very hard evidence of displeasure with their patron saint of the Autumn and the long weary Winter.

The Widow must have known all this. Not that Sandy had said a word further than she had almost forced him to speak; not that she had yet ventured down into the Forks, or that Bunker Hill had breathed a word about it, but I fancy that women know these things by instinct. They somehow have a singularly clear way of coming upon such things.

Day after day she read Sandy's face as he came up from his mine, dripping with the yellow water spurted from the sluice all over his broad slouch hat, long brown beard, and stiff duck breeches; she read it eagerly as one reads the papers after a battle, and read it truly as if it had been a broadsheet in print, and found herself in disfavor with the camp.

Then she began to think if Sandy was thinking of his promise; if he had remembered, and still remembered the time when in her great agony he promised, though all the world turned against her and cried "shame!" he would not upbraid her.

She wondered if he ever wished he had gone when she commanded him and implored him to go, and she began to read his face for the truth. She read, read him all through, page after page, chapter after chapter. She found there was not a doubt in all the realm of his soul, and her face took on again a little of its gladness. Yet the touch of tenderness deepened, the old sadness had settled back again, and this time to remain.

The still blue skies of California were bending over the camp. Not a cloud sailed east or west, or hovered about the snow-peaks. It was full Summer-time in the Sierras before it was yet mid-Spring, and men began to pour over the mountains across the settled and solid banks of snow. Birds flew low and idly about the cabins, and sang as the men went on with their work down in the foaming, muddy little rivers, and all the world seemed glad and strong with life and hope.

Still the Widow was glad no more, and men began to notice that Sandy did not come to town at all. It was even observed that he had found a cut-off across the spur of the hill, by which he went and came to and from his mining claim without once setting foot in the Howling Wilderness, or even the Forks.

Limber Tim, too, seemed sad and sorely troubled. Sunshine and singing birds do not always bring delight to all. There is nothing so sad as sadness at such a time.

CHAPTER XXIII.

ANOTHER WEDDING AT THE FORKS.

LIMBER Tim no longer wrestled with saplings or picket-fences, or even his limber legs. He had other and graver matters on hand. The birds were building their nests all about him, and he too wanted to gather moss.

At last the boy-man was happy. At least, he came one night very late to "Sandy's," as the Widow's home was now called, and standing outside of the house and backing up against the fence, and sticking his hands in behind him, and twisting his left leg around the right, he called out to Sandy in a voice that was wild and uncertain as a wind that is lost in the trees.

Sandy laid it down tenderly, covered it up, and watching it a minute and making sure that it was sound asleep and well, went out. Limber Tim was writhing and twisting more than ever before. Sandy was glad, for he now knew that he was perfectly well, and that he had got the great matter settled, and that in a way perfectly satisfactory to himself.

And yet the two men were terribly embarrassed. What made the embarrassment very much the worse was the fact that they were at least half-a-mile from the nearest saloon. Fortunately it was very dark for a Californian night, and the men could look each other in the face without seeing each other.

There was a long and painful silence. Limber Tim wrestled with his right leg with all his might, and would have thrown it time and again, but from the fact that his two arms were thrust in behind and wound through the palings, so that it was impossible for him to fall.

His mouth was open and his tongue was out, but he could not talk. At last Sandy broke the prolonged and profound silence.

"Win her, Limber?"

"Won her, Sandy."

"Bully for Limber Tim!"

Then there was another painful silence, and Limber Tim twisted a paling off the fence with his arms, and kicked half the bark off his right shin with his left boot-heel.

"Sandy?"

"Limber."

Then Limber Tim reached out his tongue and spun it about as if it had been a fish-line, and he was fishing in the darkness for words. At last he jerked back as if he had got a bite, jerked and jerked as if his throat was full of fish-hooks, and jerked till he jerked himself loose from the fence; and poising on his heel before falling back into the darkness, and twisting himself down the hill, said this:

"Git the Judge, Sandy. Fetch her home to-morrow. Spliced to-morrow. Sandy, git the Judge to-morrow!"

And "to-morrow" kept coming up the hill and out of the darkness till the nervous man was half way to the Howling Wilderness.

The Judge was there, a cooler man now, even though it was midsummer. His shirt was open till his black hairy breast showed through as if it had been a naked bear-skin.

The Forks came in force to its second wedding, but the Forks, too, was cooler, and had put aside to some extent its faith and its folly. And yet it liked Bunker Hill ever so much. Bunker Hill, said the Forks, had not been the best of women in days gone by, but Bunker Hill had never deceived.

She stood alone there that day, the day of all days to any woman in the world, and the boys did not like it at all.

Why had she not asked the Widow to be by her side? Surely she had stood by the Widow in the day of trouble; why was not the Widow there? And then they thought about it a little while, and saw how impossible it was for poor deformed little Bunker Hill to dare to ask the Widow to come and stand with her at her wedding.

The woman who stood there, about to be made the head of the second family in the Forks, had nursed the Widow back to life and health, had seen all the time the line that lay between them, and had not taken a single step to cross it. When her task was finished she had gone back to her home. She carried with her the memory and the recollection of a duty well performed, and felt that it was enough. She had not seen the Widow any more.

The Judge stood there with the Declaration of Independence, the Statutes of California, and the marriage ceremony, all under his arm, and ready to do his office. The sun was pouring down in the open streets. Little Bunker Hill felt hardly, somehow, that she had a right to be married out in the open day, in the fresh, sweet air, and under the trees; and Limber Tim preferred to be married where his partner had been married, and so it was that they had met in the Howling Wilderness as before. All was silence now, all were waiting for the Judge to begin. Up in the loft the mice nibbled away at their endless rations of old boots, and a big red-headed woodpecker pounded away on the wall back by the chimney without.

There was a commotion at the door. Then there was a murmur of admiration and applause.

The men gave way, they pushed and pushed each other back as if they had been pushing cotton bales, they opened a line, and down that line a beautiful woman with her eyes to the ground and a baby in her arms moved on till she came and stood by the side of the little hunchback, still silent, and looking with the old look of sad, sweet tranquility upon the ground.

It was really too much for the little man, who had opened his bosom, and who all the time had stood there with his books under his arm, perfectly cool, and perfect master of the situation. Now he was all of a heap. He had been acting with a sort of condescension toward the two half-children who had come before him that day, and had even prepared a sort of patronizing, half-missionary, half-reformatory sermon, but now, and all suddenly, he was utterly overthrown. He began to perspire and choke on the spot.

The silence was painful. The woodpecker pounded as if he would knock the house down, and the mice rasped at their old boots and rattled away like men sawing wood.

The Judge began to hear himself breathe.

In this moment of crisis he caught a book from his side and proceeded to read. He read from "An Act to amend an Act entitled an Act for the improvement of the breed of sheep in the State of California." Back in the saloon there were men who began to giggle. These were some men not from Missouri. They were of the hatchet-faced order, men who spoke through their noses, "idecated men," the camp called them, and men that, above all others, had put the little Judge in terror.

When he heard the men laugh, then he knew he had opened his book at the wrong place, and his face grew red as fire. He could not see to read to the end, nor could he now be heard. He suddenly closed the book and said, "Then by virtue of the authority in me vested, and under the laws of the State of California in such cases made and provided, I pronounce you man and wife."

Then the little Judge came up, shook them both by the hand, and his voice was suddenly clear as a bell, and he felt that he could now go on and speak by the hour.

The Widow bowed down above her baby and kissed the new-made bride silently and tenderly as if she had been her sister, and then with the same sweet, half sad smile she turned to the door, her face still to the ground, and covering up the little sleeper in her arms and looking neither right nor left, went back alone to her cabin.

The dark day was over. At the play, whenever you see the whole force of the company come forward and stand in a row, and assume the most striking and imposing attitudes, and hear the fiddlers play and the brass trumpets bray as never before, then you may be very sure the tragedy is about over. So it goes in life.

The crowd had melted away a bit because it was very warm, and then the men were getting noisy enough, for this was the day on which every true American was expected to get drunk. It was a sort of Fourth of July.

The old question was being again raised: The bride was standing there in the midst of the men, a true good woman, a woman who had sinned, yet a woman who had suffered. One who had fallen was she, yet one who had resisted more than many a woman who would have cast a stone at her. She was very glad, and not a man but was glad to see it.

"That baby! It is an angel, and its mother's name is Madonna. That little bit of a brat! Why, I seed it first, first of any body, and it was n't bigger than a pound of soap after a whole day's washing. Make a fuss about that little thing! A man who would make a fuss about a baby no bigger than that, no matter when it was born, is a fool!"

"Bully for Bunk — for — for Missis Tim! Bully for Missis Tim!" and the men shouted, and Mrs. Tim blushed from sheer joy.

The Gopher cheered perhaps more lustily than any one, for he admired the Widow, and knew her love and worth. The Gopher, it is true, was in disgrace, for the story went that the young man, his partner, who was the first to be buried in the Forks, had fallen by his hand. The blow had been struck in a crowd, it was said, and no one saw it, or at least no one cared to tell of it if he did, and so the Gopher had been left alone, and he had left men alone, and lived all the time by himself in a sort of cave, and that is why he was called the Gopher. Strange stories were told of this Gopher, too, and men who pretended to know said his cave was lined with gold.

"That baby!" began the Gopher, lifting up his doubled fist, and bringing it down now and then by way of emphasis. "That baby! Look here! Here's one baby among a thousand men. Here's a thousand men asking if it's got a father. Now does that little baby want a father? I've got a cave full of gold and I'll be its father! I'll be its brother and uncle and aunt and mother!" The Gopher thundered his fist down on the bar as he concluded, and the glasses there jumped up and clinked together, and bowed to each other, as if they had been dancers about to begin a cotillion.

The woodpecker flew away, and the mice were heard no more that day, for the men shouted their approval till they were hoarse-voiced as mules.

Deboon had been sitting there all the time, half doubled over a bench. He perhaps was thinking of the first wedding, for he kept looking straight across the room to the pine logs on the other side, and then he seemed to fix his eyes on some object there, and to fall to thinking very generally. At last he began to count on his fingers. Then suddenly he fairly laughed with delight. He sprang up, stepped across the room, put his finger on the spot where Limber Tim had stood scrawling with his big pencil the day he was so embarrassed at Sandy's wedding, and shouted out —

"Look here! There it is. That's the date. That's the day they was married — September eighteen hundred and fifty!"

"Just eight months!" roared a man in the crowd.

"Eight months! Ten of 'em!" and he fell to counting on his fingers, as he turned to the crowd and continued right on up to July, with perfect confidence.

The camp roared, and shouted, and danced, as never before. Why had it been so stupid as not to set this thing right from the first? It was the most penitent community that had ever been. The Widow was once more its patron saint.

The Gopher stood up by the wall.

"Are you all satisfied now?"

Satisfied! They would never doubt any woman any more as long as they lived.

He took his bowie-knife while the crowd turned to take a drink, and cut the date from the wall; and the only record, perhaps, of the first marriage in the Sierras was no more.

The sharp-nosed man, one of those miserable men who never are satisfied unless they are either miserable or making some one else so, came up to the wall out of the crowd and began to look on the wall for the date, as if he thought there might have been some mistake, and he wanted to count it all over again.

This man began to count on his fingers and to look along on the wall. Suddenly there was a something gleaming in his face like a flash of lightning.

It was the Gopher's bowie-knife. It was within two inches of his throat.

"Are you satisfied, my friend?" smiled the Gopher, with a smile that meant brimstone.

"Perfectly satisfied," said the wretch in return, and at the same time he bowed and backed as fast as he could till he came to the door, and then he was seen no more.

"Be it really all on the square, Judge?" asked Citizen Tim one day, timidly and in confidence.

"Right?—didn't I marry 'em?"

"But it war n't twelve months."

"Twelve months! don't care ef it war n't six months. I married 'em, and I married 'em good and fast, and that's the end of it."

Public opinion flows and ebbs like the tide of the sea. At one time this little camp was unanimous in the opinion that the mysterious little woman could be none other than Nancy Williams, and it would talk of little else. Then it would tire of this subject, change its opinion, and let the matter drop for months together.

CHAPTER XXIV.

THE JUDGE IS LONESOME.

"In the Spring a young man's fancy lightly turns to thoughts of love."

THIS was the song of the fat little Judge, one fine morning, as he wandered down towards the Howling Wilderness, sniffing the glorious balm, the very breath of the forest, and glancing ever and anon over his shoulder towards the cabin of Captain Tommy.

How new, and fresh and sweet, and fragrant the odors of the mighty, mossy woods that climbed and climbed and ever climbed as if to mount the summits, and push their tasselled tops against the indolent summer clouds that hovered like great white-winged birds above the peaks of snow. So new and fresh it seemed that summer morning, that the little Judge stopped on the hillside and stood there to inhale its sweetness.

"How fresh and fine is this new world of Californy. It is only finished to day. I can smell the varnish on it."

The Judge took out his great cotton bandanna, took off his hat, and polished his bald head till it shone in the sun like a mirror.

Then the little man stuffed his big handkerchief back in his bosom, and went on down the trail, humming softly to himself:

"In the Spring a young man's fancy lightly turns to thoughts of love."

A man in great gum boots, duck breeches, a hat like a tent, with a gold pan under his arm and a pipe sticking out through a mask of matted beard, met the little man in the trail, heard his song as he passed, and looking back over his shoulder, said to himself: "The derned bald-headed old rooster! What 's he a-singin hymns fur now?"

The little Judge could not sit down in the saloon. He felt that something was the matter, and he thought that he was lonesome. The little brown mice upstairs could be heard all day now, for the miners were at work up to their thighs in the water, delving away there in their great gum boots as if they were in a sort of diving-bell.

So the Judge went away from the Howling Wilderness. There was no man to be found who had time to talk, and so he sought a woman.

Captain Tommy stood in the door of her cabin all untroubled. She had seen the little

Judge approach, but she was too happy drinking in the great summer's day that filled all things with peace and a calm delight, and she did not stir.

There are days and occasions when even the most plain women are positively beautiful; and when a plain woman is beautiful she is the most beautiful thing in the world.

This was Captain Tommy's day to be beautiful, and perhaps she felt it, for there she stood, really playing the coquette, hardly turning her eyes to look on the little Alcalde, although she knew he was mad in love with her.

He stood before her in the sun with his hat in his hand. Then she looked into the polished mirror which he humbly bowed before her, and she saw that she was really beautiful.

"Captain," said the mirror, and it bowed still lower. "Lady, in this glorious climate of Californy, I have snatched a few moments from my professional duties to come to you, to say to you — to — to beg of you that you will — will you — in this glorious climate of Californy this morning?"

The mirror was close up under her eyes. She smiled, and then she lifted her two hands and began to wind herself up as fast as possible, so that she could answer the eager and earnest little man before her.

The Judge waited in an ecstacy of delight, for he knew by the twinkle in her eye that he should have to send for the black-clad man with the white necktie, who had so terrified the Parson, and he was very happy.

CHAPTER XXV.

AFTER THE DELUGE — WHAT THEN?

BY slow degrees, no one knew just when or how, the boy-poet began to find his way back after a year or two to the Widow's cabin. The miners wondered that Sandy did not protest. They saw, with some alarm, that the Widow was even more kind to him than before. Was it the pale pleading face of the consumptive boy that moved her?

Years went by, and the chronicler stood again in the Forks. The town was gone; the miners had uprooted its very foundations. Then came floods and buried the boulders and the banks of the stream, and widened it out and made it even as a new-plowed field.

Then a man, the Hon. Mr. Sandy, who had sat down with his family quite satisfied in the Sierras, extended a fence around the site of the old city, and planted and sowed and then reaped the richest of harvests. On the site of the Howling Wilderness the yellow golden grain reached up till it touched the very beard of the giant. So do perish the mining towns of the Sierras.

The hills are not so wild now; the woods have been mown away, and up on the hill-sides the miners have sat down, old and wrinkled and few in numbers; and around their quiet old cabins have planted fruit trees, and trees even from the tropics. And these trees flourish here too, for though the snow falls deep, and the sun has little room between the walls of the mighty cañon, still it seems never now so bleak or cold.

There is one little house on the hill-side, with porches, and Spanish verandahs, and hammocks swinging there, and all that, nestled down among the fruit-trees that bend with fruit and blossom. Around this cabin and back of it, and up the mountains among the firs, you see pretty children passing in and out, laughing as they run, shouting like little Modocs, shaking back their hair all full of the gold and glory of the California sun, and making every one happy who beholds them.

"All in the glorious climate of Californy!" says the little man, as he comes puffing up the hill to his home, and the children of the First Families run to meet him.

Can it be possible? Did they all grow young again? Did they go back and begin life at the beginning? Truly, there is something in the climate, and the fountain of youth flows certainly somewhere out of the Sierras.

For look! there stands a woman winding herself up to welcome her husband; she is only a little stouter, and is even beautiful.

As for Limber Tim, being an "idecated man," he started a newspaper in the nearest town, and after many battles and many defeats, finally climbed high on the ladder of distinction, and is now "the Hon. Mr. Tim," with a political influence second in that part of the country to no man, and to only one woman.

How things are changed, to be sure! The caravans of clouds that little Billie Piper was wont to look up to and wonder at, still cross the cañon, and march and countermarch and curl about the far snow peaks as before. But the coyote has ceased to howl from the hill-side.

And what can that be curling like steam up from out the mighty forest that belts the snow peaks about the heads of the three little streams that make the Forks?

It looks like a train of clouds driven straight through the tree tops—it is so high and fairy-like and far away. It is as if it were on the very summit of the Sierras.

Ah! that is the engine blowing off the clouds of steam as she drops, shoots, slides, glides from the mountain to the sea. The train is a mile in length. The dust of three thousand miles is on her skirts. But before the going down of the sun she will draw rein to rest by the Golden Gate.

CHAPTER XXVI.

THE WIDOW IN DISGRACE.

STICK a pin here. Be sure you remember that these settlers of the Sierras were as distinct a people from the settlers by the sea as you can conceive. The one was of the West, the other of the East. The one ate codfish and had a nasal accent and sang hymns. The other had never seen the ocean, he detested codfish, ate bacon and swore like a pirate.

Years went by and people, strangers, came and went, but our First Fam'lies of the Sierras remained.

This is history. The Phœnicians landed and left their impress on Ireland long before England heard of the first Cæsar. Their impetuous blood signalizes the Fenian of to-day.

The Pilgrim Fathers refused to return. A world of immigration flowed to and fro. But these few gave to the bleak and barren East the sharp nose, the nationality, good or bad, of the north of North America; while the few first settlers of the South gave spring to a current that will flow on for a thousand years.

I am all the time wondering when I think of the people of the Sierras, what women, or men and women, the traveler of a century hence will find there.

I think he will not find a coward or a miser. I think he will find a brave, generous, open-handed and unsuspicious people. A people full of freedom, of lofty aspiration, of purity, partaking of the awful sublimity that environs them.

And somewhere in these Sierras will they name the new Parnassus. The nine sisters, in the far New Day, will have their habitation here when the gold hunter has gone away, and the last pick lies rusting in the mine.

The sea of seas shall rave and knock at the Golden Gate, but this shall be the vine-land, the place of rest, that the old Greeks sought forever to find. This will be the land of eternal afternoon.

A land born of storm and rounded into shape by the blows of hardy and enduring men, it shall have its reaction — its rest.

The great singer of the future, born of the gleaming snows and the gloomy forests of the Sierras, shall some day swing his harp in the wind and move down these watered and wooded slopes to conquer the world with a song for Peace.

Now you would have me say that we never once sinned in this Eden of ours in the Sierras.

There is an old and a beautiful story. You knew it long before you learned to read. It was in that other Eden. There the living God spake face to face with man. He visited him every day in his own form. And yet he fell. We do not claim to be much better than they were in Eden, even in the Sierras.

The Forks, like every other place in the world, had its little center of Aristocracy. There was here, as in any other little community, one leading woman of fashion; the one tyrant who admitted this or that one to the Social Center. This woman, an ancient "School-marm," had firmly set her face against the Widow from the first. From this there was no appeal. The Widow was in disgrace. Still she refused to banish the boy-poet from her presence.

The old suspicion hung in the minds of the miners at the Forks. One day there were two old men, made mellow from the juice of grapes they had planted and grown on the hill-sides about their cabins, who grimly wagged their heads and looked wise at the mention of "the

Widow," as she was still called, and sympathized with Sandy.

"Yes, pra'ps it was and pra'ps it wasn't," one would say as he thought of little "Half-a-pint," now a noisy little tom-boy filling the fir woods with laughter, "but then her having that 'ere poet about her all the time, that's what sticks in my crop."

"That's what sticks in my crop," echoes his fellow, as he pushes the bushy beard from his mouth and lifts his gourd of wine.

"The reputation of this ere camp," says another, as he sets down his empty gourd and lays his fore-finger in his palm, and settles his head wisely to one side, "the reputation of this ere camp depends on a havin' of this ere thing cleared up about the Widder."

"It looks pesky black," put in the other garrulous old woman in duck breeches, "'Cause why? she still sees him."

"And Sandy?"

Three old heads, helpless, good-natured old women, who had spent their manhood and their strength long before their grape-vines were growing on the hill-side, huddled close together in half maudlin conversation.

"Sandy!"

"He's a chuckle-headed old idiart."

"He 's a gitten old and he can't help hisself."

"He 's a gitten old."

"The chuckle-headed old idiart."

"Lookee here!"

An old forty-niner rose half way up, felt that his spine was not very reliable, and so spread out his two great hands on the two shoulders of his boon companion, and peered down in his face till their two beards, white as foam, almost flowed together.

"Let 's run 'im out!"

At these words an old crippled man suddenly started up from his place back in the corner, and tottered forward to where the three old heads were huddled together.

"Run out Billie! Little Billie Piper, that never gits any older, never has a beard! that come here, that come — when did little Billie Piper come? Gintlemen, you listen to me. When you run out little Billie Piper, by God, you run him out over my bones!" And here the Gopher thundered his two fists down on to the pine-board table, and turning on his heel tottered out and up the hill-side to his cabin.

CHAPTER XXVII.

BILLIE PIPER AND DEBOON.

IT is more than possible that we, in America, did once have a real Bourbon amongst us. If a Bonaparte could come and wed with us, and cast his fortune with us, why certainly a very heir to the crown of France might come and spend his life with us, live and die unknown. I do n't know that we ever had any kings, or sons of kings, or daughters of kings, or any thing of the kind with us in the little Eden of the Sierras, but I do know that we had some odd men there, and some great men too, men that deserved to be kings, whatever they may have been.

And what they were, what they had been, no man ever knew. There was a truce to investigation. The family tree stood in the form of a sombre pine at each man's cabin door. That was enough. You could not go outside of the camp for inquiry. The eternal girdle of snow lifted its front in everlasting protest. How then shall I tell you who this silent widow that refused to go away, that refused to surrender, that refused to open her lips — how shall I tell you who she was, why she remained, or from whence she came?

As for Billie Piper, the majority of the camp of course had long settled down to the unalterable conviction that he remained for the love of the Widow. And the camp hated him for it. He was shunned, despised, for he did not look the man; he did not even act the man. When he was insulted he did not resent it. He only held his head at such times, gave the road to all, avoided all for weeks together, went on with his work in a feeble way, for he was very feeble now, and never made answer to any one.

About this time he fell ill; or at least the report ran that he was ill. Sandy was absent on business in the valley below.

One evening the Widow was seen to enter his cabin. The camp was indignant. There were now many women in the place, and her actions did not pass unobserved.

The next day the woman, the leader of society in the little mountain metropolis, cut the Widow in the street, or rather on the hill-side, for the mining town had passed away, and there was no street now.

Two sun-bonnets, made of paste-board and

calico, that reached far out over the faces of the wearers, like the cover of a pedler's wagon, met that afternoon on the hill-side.

"It 's awful!"

"It 's just awful!"

The two covered wagons were poked up close against each other.

"She staid all night!"

"She staid with him till daylight!"

"I will cut her."

"I have cut her."

The two covered wagons parted and passed on.

You remember Deboon? Well, let us see how the California gold mines treated some of the bold fellows who once courted fortune nearly a quarter of a century ago in the Sierras. These mines were great mills. They ground men, soul and body, to powder. Time, like a great river, turned the stones, and this man, like thousands and thousands of others, was ground down to nothing.

Twenty years had now passed. Twenty terrible years, in which this brave and resolute man had dared more than Cæsar, had endured more than Ney; and he now found that the entire end of his father's name had been, somewhere in the Sierras, worn or torn away, and hid or covered up for ever in the tailings. He was now nothing but "Bab." While ground-sluicing one night, and possibly wondering what other deduction could be made and not leave him nameless, he was caught in a cave, sluiced out, and carried head-first through the flume.

This last venture wore him down to about the condition of an old quarter-coin, where neither date, name, nor nationality can be deciphered. His jaws were crushed, and limbs broken, till they lay in every direction, like the claws of a sea-crab.

They took him to the County Hospital, and there they called him "Old Bab." It was a year before he got about; and then he came leaning on a staff, with a frightful face. He had lost all spirit. He sat moodily about the hospital, and sometimes said bitter things.

One day he said of Grasshopper Jim, who was a great talker, "That man must necessarily lie. There is not truth enough in the United States to keep his tongue going for ever as it does."

One evening a young candidate told him he was going to make a speech, and very patronizingly asked him to come out and hear him. Old Bab looked straight at the wall, as if counting the stripes on the paper, then said, half to himself, "The fact of Balaam's ass making a speech has had a more demoralizing influence than any other event told in the Holy Bible; for ever since that time every lineal descendant seems determined to follow his example."

His face was never relieved by a smile, and his chin stuck out fearfully: so that one day, when Snapping Andy, who was licensed by the miners to be the champion growler of the camp, called him "Old Baboon," it was as complete as a baptismal ceremony, and he was known by no other name.

Some women visited him one evening; fallen angels—women with the trail of the serpent all over them. They gave him a pipe and money, and, above all, words of encouragement and kindness.

He moodily filled the meerschaum they had brought him, and after driving a volume of smoke through his nose, looked quietly up and said: "Society is wrong. These women are not bad women. For my part, I begin to find so much that is evil in that which the world calls good, and so much that is good in what the world calls evil, that I refuse to draw a distinction where God has not."

Then he fired a double-barrelled volley at society through his nose, and throwing out volume after volume of smoke as a sort of redoubt between himself and the world he hated, drifted silently into a tropical, golden land of dreams.

CHAPTER XXVIII.

THE GOPHER.

AND do you remember the man they called The Gopher? Poor old Gopher! His was another story. He died before Baboon found his fortune, else they might have set up together, and behind their bulldogs and grizzlies growled at the world a day or two with perfect satisfaction. But fate said otherwise.

The Gopher had always been misunderstood, even from the first. If the camp held him at arm's length in the old days, it, as a rule, shunned him now, when new men came in, and murder began to be a word with a terrible meaning, and even the good Widow almost forgot him.

The camp went down, and cabins were deserted by hundreds. But there was one cabin that was never vacant; it stood apart from town, on the brown hill-side, and as it was one of the first, so it promised to be the last of the camp. It always had an ugly bull-dog tied to the door—was itself a low, suspicious-looking structure that year by year sank lower as the grass grew taller around it, till it seemed trying to hide in the chaparral. It had but one occupant, a silent, selfish man, who never came out by day except to bury himself alone in his claim at work. Nothing was known of him at all, save the story that he had killed his partner in a gambling-house away back somewhere in '51. He was shunned and feared by all, and he approached and spoke to no one except the butcher, the grocer, and expressman; and to these only briefly, on business. I believe, however, that the old cripple, Baboon, sometimes sat on the bank and talked to the murderer at work in his claim. It was even said that Baboon was on fair terms with the dog at the door.

This solitary man of the savage dog was, as you guess, "The Gopher." That was not the name given him by his parents, but it was the name the camp had given him a generation before, and it was now the only name by which he was known. The amount of gold which he had hoarded and hidden away in that dismal old cabin, through years and years of incessant toil, was computed to be enormous.

Year after year the grass stole farther down from the hill-tops to which it had been driven, as it were, in the early settlement of the camp;

at last it environed the few remaining cabins, as if they were besieged, and it stood up tall and undisturbed in the only remaining trail. Still regularly three times a day the smoke curled up from the Gopher's cabin, and the bull-dog kept unbroken sentry at the door.

In the January spring that followed, the grass and clover crept down strong and thick from the hills, and spread in a pretty carpet across the unmeasured streets of the once populous and prosperous camp. Little gray horned toads sunned themselves on the great flat rocks that had served for hearth-stones, and the wild hop-vines clambered up and across the toppling and shapeless chimneys.

About this time a closely-contested election drew near. It was a bold and original thought of a candidate to approach the Gopher and solicit his vote. His friends shook their heads, but his case was desperate, and he ventured down upon the old gray cabin hiding in the grass and chaparral. The dog protested, and the office-seeker was proceeding to knock his ugly teeth down his throat with a pick-handle, when the door opened, and he found the muzzle of a double-barrelled shot-gun in his face. The candidate did not stay to urge his claims, and the Gopher's politics remained a mystery.

Here in this land of the sun the days trench

deep into the nights of northern countries, and birds and beasts retire before the sunset: a habit which the transplanted Saxon declines to adopt.

Some idlers sat at sunset on the verandah of the last saloon, looking down the gulch as the manzanita smoke curled up from the Gopher's cabin.

There is an hour when the best that is in man comes to the surface; sometimes the outcroppings are not promising of any great inner wealth; but the indications, whatever they may be, are not false. It is dulse and drift coming to the surface when the storm of the day is over. Yet the best thoughts are never uttered; often because no fit words are found to array them in; oftener because no fit ear is found to receive them.

How lonesome it looked, that little storm-stained cabin thus alone, stooping down, hiding away in the long strong grass, as if half-ashamed of the mournful history of its sad and lonely occupant.

A sailor broke silence: "Looks like a Feejee camp on a South Sea island."

"Robinson Crusoe — the last man of the original camp — the last rose of Summer." This was said by a young man who had sent some verses to the *Hangtown Weekly*.

"Looks to me, in its crow's nest of chaparral, like the lucky ace of spades," added a man who sat apart contemplating the wax under the nail of his right forefinger.

The schoolmaster here picked up the ace of hearts, drew out his pencil and figured rapidly.

"There!" he cried, flourishing the card, "I put it an ounce a day for eighteen years, and that is the result." The figures astonished them all. It was decided that the old miser had at least a mule-load of gold in his cabin.

"It is my opinion," said the new Squire, who was small of stature, and consequently insolent and impertinent, "he had ought to be taken up, tried, and hung for killing his pardner in '51."

"The time has run out," said the Coroner, who now came up, adjusting a tall hat to which he was evidently not accustomed; "the time for such cases by the law made and provided has run out, and it is my opinion it can 't be did."

Not long after this it was discovered that the Gopher was not at work. Then it came out that he was very ill, and that Old Baboon was seen to enter his cabin.

CHAPTER XXIX.

A NATURAL DEATH.

EARLY one frosty morning in the Fall following, Old Baboon sat by the door of the only saloon. He held an old bull-dog by a tow-string, and both man and dog were pictures of distress as they shivered from the keen cold wind that came pitching down from the snow-peaks. As a man approached, the man shivered till his teeth chattered, and clutching at the string, looked helplessly over his shoulder at the uncompromising bar-keeper, who had just arisen and opened the door to let out the bad odors of his den.

The dog shivered too, and came up and sat down close enough to receive the sympathetic hand of Old Baboon on his broad bowed head. This man was a relic and a wreck. More than twenty years of miner's life and labor in the mountains, interrupted of late only by periodical sprees governed in their duration solely by the results of his last "clean up," had made him one of a type of men known only to the Pacific.

True, he had failed to negotiate with the savage cinnamon-headed vendor of poison; but he was no beggar. It was simply a failure to obtain a Wall Street accommodation in a small way. I doubt if the bristled-haired bar-keeper himself questioned the honesty of Baboon. It was merely a question of ability to pay, and the decision of the autocrat had been promptly and firmly given against the applicant.

Perhaps, in strict justice to the red-haired wretch that washed his tumblers and watched for victims that frosty morning, I should state that appearances were certainly against Baboon.

You can with tolerable certainty, in the placer mines, tell how a miner's claim is paying by the condition and quality of his top-boots. Baboon had no boots, only a pair of slippers improvised from old rubbers, and between the top of these and the legs of his pantaloons there was no compromise across the naked, cold-blue ankles.

These signs, together with a buttonless blue shirt that showed his hairy bosom, a frightful beard and hair beneath a hat that drooped like a wilted palm-leaf, were the circumstantial evidences from which Judge Barkeep made his decision.

It would perhaps be more pleasant for us all

if we could know that such men were a race to themselves; that they never saw civilization; that there never was a time when they were petted by pretty sisters, and sat, pure and strong, the central figures of Christian households; or at least we would like to think that they grew upon the border, and belonged there. But the truth is, very often, they came of the gentlest blood and life. The border man, born and bred in storms, never gets discouraged: it is the man of culture, refinement, and sensitive nature who falls from the front in the hard-fought battles of the West.

This man's brow was broad and full; had his beard and hair been combed and cared for, his head had looked a very picture. But after all, there was one weak point in his face. He had a small, hesitating nose.

As a rule, in any great struggle involving any degree of strategy and strength, the small nose must go to the wall. It may have pluck, spirit, refinement, sensitiveness, and, in fact, to the casual observer, every quality requisite to success; but somehow invariably at the very crisis it gives way.

Small noses are a failure. This is the verdict of history. Give me a man, or woman either, with a big nose — not a nose of flesh, not a loose flabby nose like a camel's lips, nor a thin, starved nose that the eyes have crowded out and forced into prominence, but a full, strong, substantial nose, that is willing and able to take the lead; one that asserts itself boldly between the eyes, and reaches up towards the brows, and has room enough to sit down there and be at home.

Give me a man, or woman either, with a nose like that, and I will have a nose that will accomplish something. I grant you that such a nose may be a knave; but it is never a coward nor a fool — never!

In the strong stream of miners' life as it was, no man could stand still. He either went up or down. The strong and not always the best went up. The weak — which often embraced the gentlest and sweetest natures — were borne down and stranded here and there all along the river.

I have noticed that those who stop, stand, and look longest at the tempting display of viands in cook-shop windows, are those that have not a penny to purchase with. Perhaps there was something of this nature in Old Baboon that impelled him to look again and again over his shoulder — as he clutched tighter to the tow-string — at the cinnamon-headed bottle-washer behind the bar.

A stranger stood before this man. He

turned his eyes from the barkeeper and lifted them helplessly to his.

"Charlie is dead."

"Charlie who? Who is 'Charlie'?"

"Charlie Godfrey, The Gopher, and here is his dog;" and as he spoke, the dog, as if knowing his master's name and feeling his loss, crouched close to the old man's legs.

A new commotion in camp.

Say what you will of gold, whenever any one shuts his eyes and turns for ever from it, as if in contempt, his name, for a day at least, assumes a majesty proportionate with the amount he has left behind and seems to despise.

CHAPTER XXX.

A FUNERAL.

THE Coroner, who was a candidate for a higher office, marshalled the leading spirits, and proceeded to the cabin where the dead man lay. He felt that his reputation was at stake, and entering the cabin, said in a solemn voice: "In the name of the law, I take possession of this primesis." Some one at the door, evidently not a friend to the Coroner's political aspirations, called out: "O what a hat!" The officer was not abashed, but towered up till his tall hat touched the roof, and repeated, "In the name of the law, I take possession of these primesis." This time there was no response or note of derision, and it was quietly conceded that The Gopher and all his gold were in the hands of the Coroner.

The cabin was a true and perfect relic of what might, geologically speaking, be termed a "Period" in the plastic formation of the Republic. Great pine logs, one above the other, formed three of its walls; the fourth was made up by a fire-place, constructed of boulders and adobe. The bed had but one post; a pine slab, supported by legs set in the center of the earthen floor, formed a table; the windows were holes, chiseled out between the logs, that could be closed with wooden plugs in darkness or danger.

Let these cabins not be despised. Their builders have done more for the commerce of the world than is supposed.

It is to be admitted that the dead man did not look so terrible, even in death, as the mind had pictured him. His unclosed eyes looked straight at those who came only to reproach him, and wonder where his money was buried, till they were abashed.

Standing there, the jury, under direction of the Coroner, gave a verdict of "Death from general debility." Some one tried to bring the Coroner into contempt again, by afterwards calling attention to the fact that he had forgotten to swear the jury; but the officer replied, "It is not necessary in such cases by the law made and provided," and so was counted wise and correct.

They bore the body in solemn silence to the grave yard on the hill—may be a little nearer to heaven. "How odd, that nearly all grave yards are on a hill," said little Billie Piper once more. But he said it now to himself, for he stood alone. No one shook hands with him now. He had crept out of his bed to stand by his dead friend. The places of chief mourners were assigned to Baboon and the dog, and Billie Piper. Whether these places were given because Baboon and Billie were the only present friends of the deceased, or whether the dog quietly asserted a right that no one cared to dispute, is not certain. Most likely it was one of those things that naturally, and therefore correctly, adjust themselves.

When these bearded men in blue shirts rested their burden at the open grave, they looked at each other, and there was an unpleasant pause. Perhaps they thought of the Christian burial-service in other lands, and felt that something was wanting. At last Baboon stole up close to the head of the grave, hesitated, lifted and laid aside his old slouch hat, and looking straight down into the earth, said, in a low and helpless way:

"Earth to earth and dust to dust!" — hesitated again and then continued: "The mustard and the clover seed are but little things, and no man can tell the one from the other; yet bury them in the uttermost parts of the earth, and each will bring its kind perfect and beautiful,— and — and — man is surely more than a little seed — and — and ;" here he quite broke down, and knelt and kissed the face of the dead.

The men looked away for a while, as if to objects in the horizon, and then, without looking at each other, or breaking silence, lowered the unshapely box, caught up the spades, and found a relief in heaping the grave.

Then the Coroner, as in duty bound, or, as he expressed it, "as required by the law in such cases made and provided," directed his attentions to a search for the buried treasure.

Yeast-powder boxes, oyster-cans, and sardine-boxes, old boots and quicksilver tanks, were carried out to the light and inspected, without results. "In the straw of the bunk," said the Coroner;— and blankets, bunk, and straw were carried out to the sun ; but not an ounce of gold.

To make sure against intrusion of the ill-disposed, the unwearied Coroner slept on the spot. The next day the hearth was taken up carefully, piece by piece, but only crickets clad in black, and little pink-eyed mice met the eager eyes of the men. At last some one suggested that as the hard-baked earthen floor was the last place in which one would look for hidden treasures, that was probably the first and only place in which the Gopher had buried his gold.

The thought made the Coroner enthusiastic. He sent for picks, and, if we must tell the truth, and the whole truth, he sent for whisky also. By sunset the entire earthen floor had been dug to the depth of many feet, and emptied outside the door. Not a farthing's-worth of gold was found. The next day the chimney was taken down.

Lizards, dust of adobes, but nothing more. About this time, the memory of the man just taken to the hill was held in but little respect, and a good or bad name, so far as the over-zealous Coroner was concerned, depended entirely on the final results of the search.

But one more thing remained to be done; that was, to remove the cabin. Shingle by shingle, log by log, the structure was levelled. Wood-rats, kangaroo-mice, horned toads, a rattlesnake or two that had gone into winter-quarters under the great logs, and that was all. Not an ounce of gold was found in the last cabin of the Missouri camp.

The flat was then staked off as mining-ground by some enterprising strangers, and they began in the center to sluice it to the bed-rock. They sluiced up the gulch for a month, and then down the gulch for a month, until the whole hill-side was scalped, as it were, to the bone, and the treasure-hunters were bankrupt, but not even so much as the color of the dead man's gold was found.

The Forks was disgusted, and the Gopher was voted a worse man dead than living.

It began to be noticed, however, that Baboon had mended somewhat in his personal appearance since the death of the Gopher, and it was whispered that he knew where the treasure was.

Some even went so far as to say that he had the whole sum of it in his possession. "Some of these nights he'll come up a-missing," said the butcher, striking savagely at his steel across his block. In justice to The Forks it must be observed she was not without grounds to go upon in her suspicions. For was not Baboon near the man at his death? And if he could get his dog, why not get his gold also?

One night Baboon, holding tight to a tow-string, shuffled up to the stranger in the Saloon, and timidly plucking his sleeve, said:

"Going away, I hear?"

"Yes."

"To the States?"

"Yes."

"To Missouri?"

"May be."

"Well, then, look here: come with me!"—and with an old dog bumping his head against his heels, he led the way out the door down the gulch to the cabin. He pulled the latch-string, entered, and finally struck a light. Sticking the candle in a whisky-bottle that stood on a greasy table in the center of the earthen floor, he picked up the tow-string, and pointing to the bunk in the corner, they sat down together, and the old dog rested his nose between the old man's legs.

After looking about the cabin in nervous silence for a time, Baboon arose with a look of resolution, handed the man his string, stepped to a niche in the wall, and taking an old crevicing-knife, struck it in stoutly above the latch.

"This means something," said the man to himself; "here will be a revelation," and a vision of the Gopher's gold-bags crossed his mind with tempting vividness. After a while the old man came back, took up the whisky-bottle, removed the candle from its neck, and holding it up between his face and the light, which he held in the other hand, seemed to decide some weighty proposition by the run of the beads in the bottle, and then turned and offered it in silence.

As the stranger declined his kindness, he hurriedly took a long draught, replaced the candle, then came and sat down close at his side, took his string, and the old dog again thrust his nose between his knees.

"You see,"—and the man leaned over to the other, and began in a whisper and strangeness of manner that suggested that his mind was wandering,—"you see, we all came out here together: Godfrey, that's the Gopher; Wilson, that's Curly, and I. Things did n't go right with me there, after I came away, so I just let them drift here. Lost my 'grip,' as they say, did n't have any 'snap' any more, as people call it. Godfrey and Wilson got on very well, though, till Wilson was killed."

"Till the Gopher killed him?"

"Well, now, there 's where it is," said Old Baboon, and he shuddered. The dog, too, seemed to grow nervous, and crowded his ugly head up tighter between the old man's legs.

"There 's where it is. Godfrey did not kill Wilson. The Gopher did not kill Curly no more than did you. You see, Curly was young, and out here, he fell to gambling and taking a bit too much, and one night, when Godfrey tried to get him away from a game, a set of roughs got up a row, upset the table, and Curly got knifed by some one of the set, who made the row to get a grab at the money. Godfrey was holding the boy at the time to keep him from striking, for he was mad drunk.

Poor Curly only said, 'Do n't let them know it at home,' and died in his arms. Every body was stranger to every body then, and no one took stock in that which did not concern him. People said Godfrey was right — that it was a case of self-defense, and Godfrey never said a word, never denied he killed him, but went back to the cabin, and took possession of everything, and had it all his own way. He worked like a Chinaman, and never took any part in miners' meetings, or any thing of the kind, and people began to fear and shun him. By-and-by most of his old friends had gone; and he was only known as the Gopher."

Again Baboon paused, and the dog crept closer than before, as if he knew the name of his master.

Once more the man arose, lifted the candle, contemplated the beads in the bottle, as before, and returned. He did not sit down, but took up and pulled back the blankets at the end of the bunk.

"I thought as much," said the stranger to himself. "The gold is hidden in the straw."

"Look at them," said he; and he threw down a bundle of papers, and held down the dim candle.

There were hundreds of letters, all written in a fine steel-plate lady's hand. Some addressed to Godfrey, and some to Wilson. Now and then was one with a border of black, tell-ing that some one at home no longer waited the return. "Come home, come home," was at the bottom of them all. One addressed to Wilson, of a recent date, thanked him with all a mother's and sister's tenderness for the money he had so constantly sent them through all the weary years.

"That was it, you see; that was it. As Godfrey, that 's the Gopher, is dead, and can send them no more money, and as you was a-going to the States, I thought best that you should drop in and tell the two families gently, somehow, that they both are dead. Say that they died together. He sent them the last ounce he had the week before he died, and made me take these letters to keep them away from the Coroner, so that he might not know his address, and so that they might not know at home that Curly had died long ago, and died a gambler. Take one of the letters along, and that will tell you where they are."

Again Old Baboon resumed the tow-string. He looked toward the door, and when the man had stepped across the sill he put out the light, and the two stood together.

The old dog knew there was but the one place for his master outside his cabin at such a time, and, blind leading the blind, thither he led him through the dark to the saloon.

* * * * *

And whither went the Parson that cold blustering morning? He set his face against the snow and started out alone up the corkscrew trail to try to reach, no one knew where. Or did he try to reach any place at all? Did he not take this course so that he might leave the mind of the woman he had loved, free and careless of his fate?

Sandy had promised, and so he had led his new wife to the Parsonage, and taken possession as he had agreed. But rough as he was he often wished he had not done so. He could see the hand of his great rival the Parson in all things around him. Sometimes he almost fancied he could see his face, mournful, sad, looking in at the window out of the storm at the happy pair by his hearth-stone.

Early one Autumn some prospectors pushed far up the Fork running parallel with the trail leading out of camp; and there, in the leaves, they found a skull. There was a hole in the temple, and the marks of sharp teeth on the smooth white surface. They also found a small silver-mounted pistol.

The party came down to the Forks one night, where friends were enjoying themselves at the saloon. The leader told what they had found, and laid the pistol on the counter.

It was one of the Parson's little "bull-pups." The pistol was empty.

One final word of the once genteel Deboon, and we prepare to descend from the Sierras. Buffeted, beaten down, and blown about, still he lingered near his old haunts in the Forks.

At last, the broken man, who was now only known as Old Baboon, because he was so ugly, and twisted, and bent, and crooked, when he had no home, no mine, no mind, nothing at all, and did not want any thing at all but a grave, stumbled on to a mine that made him almost a prince in fortune. He would not leave the Sierras now. He settled there. Here is an extract from a letter in which he invites a distinguished traveling Yankee philanthropist and missionary to come to him and make his house his home. After describing the house and lands, he says:

"The house stands in this wood of pine. We have two California grizzlies, and a pair of bull-dogs. Sandy keeps the dogs chained, but I let the grizzlies go free. We are not troubled with visitors."

CHAPTER XXXI.

THE CARAVAN OF DEATH.

THE little poet had no place in the heart of the camp at the first. And now at the last when he was about to go away, he held even a less place than when he came.

Nobody knew when he came, nobody cared. Now that he was passing away at last, nobody, save the Widow, knew of it. Nobody cared to know of it. Truly, this singular creature did not "fit in" anywhere in the Sierras.

The Widow had been seen to enter the little hermitage alone, and very regularly of late, but no one made inquiry or interfered now. The case was peculiar. The guilt of the Widow was an accepted fact. No one under the circumstances could speak to her of him. They left this all to her, a sort of monopoly of death.

We leave her at this bedside and turn for the last time to the little Chinaman.

And what became of the little brown man with the meek almond eyes and the peaceful smile that for ever hovered about the corner of his mouth?

Poor little Washee-Washee! When the Widow got married he had to go. He could not embark in business again, and he would not go away. The Widow always gave him all he asked when he came to her, but that was very little. She even tried to persuade him to accept little gifts, and to take some delicacies for his stomach's sake, but the little pagan would only shake his head, smile the least bit out of one corner of his mouth, and then go away as if half offended.

Every five years there is a curious sort of mule caravan seen meandering up and down the mining streams of California, where Chinamen are to be found. It is a quiet train, and quite unlike those to be found there driven by Mexicans, and bearing whisky and dry goods. In this train or caravan the drivers do not shout or scream. The mules, it always seemed to me, do not even bray. This caravan travels almost always by night, and it is driven and managed almost altogether by Chinamen. These Chinamen are civil, very respectful, very quiet, very mournful both in their dress and manner.

These mules, both in coming in and in going out of a camp, are loaded with little beech-wood boxes of about three feet in length and one foot square.

When the train arrives in a camp these boxes

are taken from off the backs of the mules, stored in some Chinaman's cabin close to the trail, and there they lie, so far as the world knows, undisturbed for two or three days. Then some midnight, the mules are quietly drawn up to the cabin-door, the boxes are brought out, and the mules are loaded, and the line winds away up the hill and out on the mountain to where their freight can be taken down to the sea on wheels.

The only apparent difference in these boxes now is the lead label at either end, which was not there when they entered the camp.

This is the caravan of the dead. No Chinaman will consent to let his bones lie in the land of the barbarian. The bones of every Chinaman, even to the beggar — if there ever was such a thing as a Chinese beggar in California — are taken back to the land of his fathers.

Washee-Washee stood watching the train climb the corkscrew trail in the gray dawn one morning, and then shaking his head he went to the Widow and said –

"By'ee, by'ee. Washee-Washee allee samee."

And it was so. His first great commercial enterprise had been a disastrous failure, and the brown little fellow never recovered. Other Chinamen poured into camp, and he certainly had friends among them all, but he went to none in his griefs as he did to the Widow; she who had been his friend in his first great trouble.

The little brown man took to opium, and gradually grew almost black. His little bright black eyes grew brighter, his thin face grew thinner, and he became a little more than a shadow. Still he would smile a bit out of that corner of his mouth. Would smile as if he was smiling at Death, and was trying to cheat him into the idea that he felt perfectly well.

The caravan came in due time; as before, it rested, loaded, climbed the hill, and as the train led up against the morning star, you might have read on one little box, wherein a skeleton lay doubled up like a jack knife, this name:

"WASHEE-WASHEE."

CHAPTER XXXII.

THE END.

PEOPLE began to remember that they had not seen their silent and singular little poet since the death and burial of the Gopher.

Surely he was ill. At all events, the Widow went boldly and regularly now to his cabin. And to the credit of the camp, be it said, it at last began to look with toleration on these missions to the humble vine-clad hermitage of the sad and lonesome little poet.

Only once more he came out and sat by the door, pale and dreamy and full of mystery.

The schoolmaster, not an unkindly man, stopped a moment with his book and slate under his arm, as he led a little girl by the hand, and looking into the palid face before him, said:

"It is a hard old world, Billie. A hard old world. At best we have to belabor the old earth; beat her to make her give us bread."

"Beat her!" The little thin hands clasped and lifted as if in prayer. "Belabor my dear mother Earth? Why, she gave us birth, she gives us all our bread, she gives us all that is beautiful and good. She will take us again to her bosom. I will pray to Earth, that I may have rest on her tranquil breast."

The schoolmaster passed on, and the sad little dreamer arose with difficulty, and passed for the last time from the light of the sun.

When the schoolmaster walked by next morning the door stood open. The little girl looked in, and then ran away as if afraid. Did she see with her child vision the face of death? The Schoolmaster, perhaps fearing to compromise his character by any association with this singular being, hurried on after the little girl, and did not turn around or look back till he had set foot over the sill of the little log school-house on the hill. His heart was beating very wildly. He had said nothing, he had heard nothing, he had seen nothing. But somehow the man's heart was beating with a strange terror, and he wanted to turn back and enter the cabin, and speak once more to the lonely little sufferer.

The man called his school to order, however, took off his coat, hung it up behind the door, ran his two hands through his hair, time and again, but failing to pacify himself by this means, called out a little boy, and flogged him soundly.

He afterwards remembered that there was

a black cat sitting in the door as he passed, quietly washing her face, yet at the same time looking intently at him out of her green eyes.

The heroes of the world are women. The women, as a rule, have done the great deeds of valor. Men, however, have written the histories and appropriated a great deal indeed to themselves.

I know very well that in a certain kind of noisy heroism man makes a great mark, and instances of valor, even in a quiet way, where man fights his battle alone and in the dark, without the observation or applause of the world, are not wanting. But the great battles, in darkness and disgrace, where death and ignominy waited, the small-great battles, the heart the battle-field, where no friend would come, where no pen should chronicle, these silent fights have been fought and won by women.

Understanding all this I can understand why the Widow chose to bear all the reproof, and let her friend, the refugee, the dreamer, the "Poet," live and die unknown and in peace.

The next morning as the Schoolmaster came by, with the little girl sliding up close to his legs, on the opposite side from the cabin, the Widow with a face of unutterable sadness was outside trying to tie a piece of something black to the door-latch.

The man lifted his hat, and came reverently and slowly forward.

There was no need of saying anything now. He understood it all, and after assisting her in silence to do the office of respect for the dead within, he took the little girl's hand again in his, turned to go, took a few steps forward, and then stopping and turning around, again lifted his hat and said softly to the Widow:

"I will stop at the saloon and send up some of the boys to take charge of the body and prepare it for the grave."

"No," sighed the Widow in a voice that was scarcely heard above the beating of her heart, "No, George," and she came slowly and calmly up to the man and stood there with her white face lifted close into his. "No George, you will go back to the house, and get your mother and your sister to come and help me now at the last. For it is a woman that lies dead there in that little vine-covered cabin."

The woman had kept the woman's secret. She had given her life as it were for the life of another. But now that all was over; the whole story was to be written in the single name on the little granite gravestone. It was the name of NANCY WILLIAMS.

THE END.

PUBLICATIONS

OF

JANSEN, McCLURG & Co.

CHICAGO, ILLINOIS.

CATON.—A Summer in Norway, with Notes on the Industries, Habits, etc., of the People, the History of the Country, the Climate and Productions, and of the Red Deer, Reindeer, and Elk, by Hon. J. D. CATON, LL.D. 8vo., 401 pages. Illustrated. Price, $2.50.

"The tone of the book is frank, almost colloquial, always communicative and leaves a favorable impression both of the intelligence and good nature with which the author pursued his way through unknown wilds. * * They are excellent specimens of terse and graphic composition, presenting a distinct image to the mind, without any superfluous details."—*New York Tribune.*

"The book of travels, which Judge CATON has presented to the public, is of a high order of merit, and sets forth the interesting natural phenomena and popular characteristics of the land of the 'unsetting sun' with great strength and clearness." —*Boston Post.*

"He is, as far as we know, the first foreign traveler who has given anything like a correct statement of the nature of the union between Norway and Sweden." —*The Nation.*

CHARD.—Across the Sea, and Other Poems. By THOS. S. CHARD. Square 16mo., 55 pages, tinted paper. Price, $1.00.

"This little gem of a book is one of the best instances of *multum in parvo* that has been furnished the reading public in a long time. * * The poetry is of a kind not often seen now-a-days; it is of the soul, and reads as though given by inspiration. * * There is a mysticism in the little book, which reminds us of the 'Lotus Eaters' or 'Festus.'"—*The Alliance.*

CLEVELAND.—Landscape Architecture, as applied to the wants of the West; with an Essay on Forest Planting on the Great Plains. By H. W. S. CLEVELAND, Landscape Architect. 16mo., 147 pages. Price, $1.00.

"My object in these few pages is simply to show that, by whatever name it may be called, the subdivision and arrangement of land for the occupation of civilized men, is an art demanding the exercise of ingenuity, judgment and taste, and one which nearly concerns the interest of real estate proprietors, and the welfare and happiness of all future occupants."—*Extract from Preface.*

CRAWFORD.—A Few Thoughts for a Few Friends. By Miss ALICE ARNOLD CRAWFORD. Square 12mo., full gilt, tinted paper, 162 pages. Price, $2.00.

"There is about these poems an air of trusting faith, of gentle tenderness, as if of one who, soaring upon the confines of a better life, had longed to leave some sweet remembrance here. They stand forth from the way-side of poetic literature like some peaceful chapel robed in ivy, where the dead are strewn with flowers, and the living steal in the shadows of the evening to seek a rest from weariness and pain."—*Inter-Ocean.*

FOYE.—Tables for the Determination and Classification of Minerals Found in the United States. By JAMES C. FOYE, A.M., Professor of Chemistry and Physics, Lawrence University, Appleton, Wisconsin. Flexible covers, 38 pages. Price, 75 cents.

"Following Dana, our chief American authority, and gathering aid from various distinguished European writers, this brief manual aims to furnish the student with such help as is needed in order to determine and classify the minerals of the United States. Some useful hints as to apparatus, and suitable notes upon other matters, precede the tables."—*Journal of Education.*

GILES.—Out from the Shadows. A Novel; by Miss ELLA A. GILES. 12mo., 317 pages. Price, $1.50.

"Miss Giles' first work has had a very large sale, and has attracted the attention of readers and critics throughout the country. Her second book gives evidence of the ripening powers of the authoress, and shows the improvement which she has made as a writer, and a mastery of style and effect which are really uncommon." —*Milwaukee News.*

"The characters are all well conceived, and the story is pleasantly written." *Inter-Ocean.*

GILES.—Bachelor Ben. A Novel; by Miss ELLA A. GILES. 12mo., 308 pages. Price, $1.50.

"A story of great descriptive and analytic mastery. * * A master-piece of free and natural handling of human life, and marks a new departure in fiction, in that the hero never marries, and the author has attempted to group the sympathies of readers about an unconventional man."—*Home Journal* (New York).

"The book is refreshingly guiltless of all superfluous characters. The tone is good throughout. The moral apparent."—*Chicago Times.*

HALL.—Poems of the Farm and Fireside. By EUGENE J. HALL. 8vo., 114 pages. Fully illustrated. Plain, price, $1.75; full gilt, price, $2.25.

"In vigor and pathos they are certainly equal—we should say superior—to Carleton's Farm Ballads; in humor scarcely inferior to the Biglow Papers."—*Interior.*

"There is a nobility of mind even among the toilers of the land too often overlooked, and for this reason we like the flavor of these poems, because they smell of the field and forest, as well as portray the inner life of society at the fireside."—*Pittsburgh Commercial.*

HEWITT.—" Our Bible." Three Lectures, delivered at Unity Church, Oak Park, Ill., by Rev. J. O. M. HEWITT. 12mo., 109 pages. Price, $1.25.

"This volume is rich in erudition and conspicuously clear in the enunciation of the objections to the orthodox idea of an inspiration which makes it infallible in all particulars."—*Chicago Journal.*

LAMARTINE.—Graziella; a Story of Italian Love. Translated from the French of A. DE LAMARTINE by JAMES B. RUNNION. Small 4to, 235 pages, red line, tinted paper, full gilt, uniform with holiday edition of "Memories." Price, $2.00.

"'Graziella' is a poem in prose. The subject and the treatment are both eminently poetic. * * * It glows with love of the beautiful in all nature. * * * It is pure literature, a perfect story, couched in perfect words. The sentences have the rythm and flow, the sweetness and tender fancy of the original. It is uniform with 'Memories,' the fifth edition of which has just been published, and it should stand side by side with that on the shelves of every lover of pure, strong thoughts put in pure, strong words. 'Graziella' is a book to be loved."—*Tribune.*

MASON.—Mae Madden. A Story; by Mrs. MARY MURDOCH MASON, with an introductory poem by JOAQUIN MILLER. 16mo., red edges. Price, $1.25.

"There is hardly a page in which you may not find some bright, fresh thought; some little generalization full of the flavor of true wit, or some charming description, deliciously feminine, and running over with the spirit of poetry."—*Cincinnati Times.*

We have read this little book with great pleasure. * * * It frequently reminds us of Mr. Howell's delicately constructed stories, and in it, as in a mirror, we see reflected that true refinement and culture of the author's mind."—*New Haven Palladium.*

MASON AND LALOR.—The Primer of Political Economy, in Sixteen Definitions and Forty Propositions, by A. B. MASON and J. J. LALOR. 12mo., 67 pages. Price, 75 cents.

"We know of no other work anywhere of sixty pages that begins to give the amount of information on the subject that has been put with such remarkable clearness into these sixty pages."—*Hartford Courant.*

"For a short and comprehensive treatise, we know of nothing better than 'The Primer of Political Economy.' The information is conveyed in a very concise and happy manner. The style is perfectly transparent, and the illustrations admirably chosen. We venture to believe that not a quarter of the men in the Lower House of Congress know as much about Political Economy as can be learned from this compact and interesting little treatise."—*Christian Register.*

MILLER.—First Fam'lies of the Sierras. A Novel; by JOAQUIN MILLER. 12mo., 258 pages. Price, $1.50.

A most graphic and realistic sketch of life in a mining cañon in the very earliest days of California. The rough heroes and heroines are evidently drawn from life, and the dramatic scenes are full of thrilling interest. Bret. Harte has never worked this rich vein of American life to better advantage.

MÜLLER.—Memories; A Story of German Love. Translated from the German of MAX MÜLLER, by GEO. P. UPTON. Small 4to., 173 pages, red-line, tinted paper, full gilt. Price, $2.00. The same, 16mo., red edges. Price, $1.00.

"'Memories' is one of the prettiest and worthiest books of the year. The story is full of that indescribable half-naturalness, that effortless vraisemblance, which is so commonly a charm of German writers, and so seldom paralleled in English. * * * Scarcely could there be drawn a more lovely figure than that of the invalid Princess, though it is so nearly pure spirit that earthly touch seems almost to profane her."—*Springfield (Mass.) Republican.*

Mc LANDBURGH.—The Automaton-Ear and Other Sketches. By MISS FLORENCE McLANDBURGH. (*In press*).

Any one of the many who have read "The Man at Crib,' "The Automaton-Ear," or "The Anthem of Judea," which have been so widely copied in various periodicals, will look with the highest anticipations to this author, who is no less gifted than she is original and eccentric.

SWING.—Truths for To-Day. *First Series.* By PROFESSOR DAVID SWING. 12mo., 325 pages, tinted paper. Price, $1.50.

"The preacher makes no display of his rich resources, but you are convinced that you are listening to a man of earnest thought, of rare culture, and of genuine humanity. His forte is evidently not that of doctrinal discussion. He deals in no nice distinctions of creed. He has no taste for hair-splitting subtleties, but presents a broad and generous view of human duty, appealing to the highest instincts and the purest motives of a lofty manhood."—*New York Tribu*

SWING.—Truths for To-Day. *Second Series.* By PROFESSOR DAVID SWING. (*In press*).

This volume will contain the latest discourses of PROF. SWING, some of them preached at the Fourth Church, but most of them spoken at the Theatre to the New Central Church. It is universally conceded that these are the finest efforts he has ever made, and the general demand for their preservation in more permanent form than the newspaper reports, has led to their issue in this volume. They are selected, revised and arranged for publication by PROF. SWING himself.

SWING.—Trial of Prof. Swing. The *Official Report* of this important trial. 8vo., 286 pages. Price, $1.75.

"It constitutes a complete record of one of the most remarkable ecclesiastical trials of modern times."—*Boston Journal.*

"This volume will be a precious bit of history twenty-five years hence, and its pages will be read with mingled interest and surprise."—*Golden Age.*

Any of the books on this list sent by mail, post-paid, on receipt of price by the publishers.

JANSEN, McCLURG & CO.
117 & 119 STATE ST., CHICAGO.

www.ingramcontent.com/pod-product-compliance
Lightning Source LLC
LaVergne TN
LVHW010241110826
845151LV00004B/1354

* 9 7 8 1 4 2 5 5 2 3 9 0 9 *